IN ANOTHER COUNTRY

Also by Susan Kenney

GARDEN OF MALICE: a mystery

IN ANOTHER COUNTRY
A Novel

SUSAN KENNEY

THE VIKING PRESS   NEW YORK / LONDON

Copyright © 1975, 1980, 1984 by Susan Kenney
All rights reserved
First published in 1984 by the Viking Press
40 West 23rd Street, New York, N. Y. 10010
Published simultaneously in Canada by
Penguin Books Canada Limited

This work was completed with the support of a grant from the National
Endowment for the Arts.

"In Another Country" appeared originally in *Boston Globe Magazine*; "Mirrors,"
"Facing Front," and "Death of the Dog and Other Rescues," in *Epoch*; "A Place
I've Never Been," in *Hudson Review*; and "Hallways," in *Ladies' Home
Journal.*

Library of Congress Cataloging in Publication Data
Kenney, Susan, 1941–
    In another country.
    I. Title.
PS3561.E44515   1984   813'.54   83.40242
ISBN 0-670-39486-6

Grateful acknowledgment is made to Mainstay Music, Inc., for
permission to reprint portions of lyrics from the song
"Everyone's Gone to the Moon," by Kenneth King. Copyright
© 1965 by Marquis Music Ltd., London, England for the
World. All rights for the USA, Canada, Japan and Mexico
controlled by Mainstay Music, Inc., 344 East 49th Street, New
York, N.Y.

Printed in the United States of America
Set in Primer

For Ed,
Who came back

CONTENTS

MIRRORS 1

A PLACE I'VE NEVER BEEN 23

FACING FRONT 51

IN ANOTHER COUNTRY 91

HALLWAYS 117

THE DEATH OF THE DOG
AND OTHER RESCUES 131

IN ANOTHER COUNTRY

MIRRORS

My father died suddenly when he was forty and I was twelve. For years after his death I was bitterly resentful of his abrupt departure: I tried to keep the memory of him, his voice, his face, the color of his hair, the way he moved, the clothes he wore, and noted the anniversary of his death each year as it came around. Five years, ten years, twelve, and he had been dead as long as I knew him; fifteen, twenty-five, the years passing so quickly that soon he would be dead as long as he had been alive. I regarded that anniversary with an almost physical dread; we are alive so little and dead so long, and even in the memories of those who want to keep us we fade away.

I never stopped feeling bereft; knowing him only as a father, I had not known him at all as a man, and I never would. My memories were so few and insignificant: when he bent down to listen to me or pick me up, his cigarettes and lighter would fall out of his breast pocket onto the floor with a clank. They always fell but he never moved them to a safer place, and that sound accompanied my growing up, until he no longer had to bend over so far to reach me.

I blamed him for never writing down his thoughts. He never wrote me a single letter, so there was no trace of him in his own words. How could anyone be so careless of his own identity? Didn't he know that he would die someday and leave me wondering? I tried to reconstruct the fragments he had left me, tried to make remembered words and movements, bits of conversation, take on coherence and show him whole. But I couldn't do it, and after a while I put my fragments away, old unsorted photographs yellowing in a dusty attic box. Then the other day I overheard a scrap of conversation. "Oh, it's all done with mirrors, you know." The phrase echoed strangely. I could hear my father saying it to me, and suddenly a whole sequence opened in my memory.

I remember getting out of my father's black company Buick into a small ditch full of dusty matted field grass along a rutted and graveled backcountry road on the outskirts of Toledo, Ohio, where we lived until 1953. My father came around the side of the car, a tall, stocky man squinting from the glare; we could not see the sun, but its light caught the dust in the air and made it glitter. He took my hand and we went up through the flattened grass into a parking lot half full of cars. I don't remember exactly what I was wearing,

probably shorts and a shirt, the detested Buster Brown ox-
fords he claimed were so good for my feet, and socks run
down into the heels, but I recall quite clearly that my father
had on a baggy gray gabardine suit, a thin white short-
sleeved shirt, and a maroon and yellow bow tie. I see him
walking absentmindedly through the ruts of the parking
lot, his wide pant legs alternately flapping and clinging
around his shins, while I leap and tug ahead.

From the parking lot I could see the huge tan circus tent
ballooning in and out with the wind, set in the flat mid-
western field as though it had grown up with the hay. The
tent and the ground were almost the same color and texture; behind them the sky hung slate-gray and opaque with
rain clouds. Dust billowed up from the grass around the
feet of the men who were still tightening the guy wires, and
it puffed around our ankles and covered our socks with
each step we took.

We passed the booth where a man was winding cotton
candy. I pleaded with my father to get me some; he screwed
up his face in disgust and muttered about it being all air
and sugar and not fit to eat, bad for my teeth, even as he
dug into his right pocket for the change. The cotton candy
man spun out a sticky wad onto the cardboard cone and
handed it to me. I tasted the flavor of the cardboard cone
and felt the rough texture of the cotton candy as it disinte-
grated against my tongue. I tried to catch a big enough
mouthful to chew on before it dissolved completely, so
sweet it hurt my teeth as it melted. My father was still muttering about cavities and your money's worth as we walked
along toward the main circus tent, but when I offered him a
bite he took it.

3

I suppose we never would have gone into the sideshow if great globules of rain hadn't begun to fall from that stony sky. Although we had gone to a lot of circuses together, my father had never taken me into the sideshow tent, and each time we passed one my curiosity grew. Always he refused with the same argument and dragged me unwilling into the big tent, where I forgot my burning desire to see the sideshow in the noise and color of the actual circus. But as we walked past the smaller tent, once again I began to plead.

"Daddy, can't we see the sideshow just this once? I'm old enough now, and you never let me."

"Sara," he said with a sigh, "I've told you that the sideshow is just another name for freaks. You don't want to go inside and stare and laugh at other people's misfortunes, do you?"

"Yes."

"But honey, it's just a come-on to make money out of vulgar curiosity, and besides, most of the things are fake."

We had stopped, and I planted my feet in front of the sideshow tent, prepared to take a stand. "Well, if they are fake, then it won't hurt to stare at them, because they aren't really misfortunes." My father looked at me blankly; I kept right on. "Besides, if you know what's inside, then you must have seen one, and if you've seen one, why can't I?"

My father smiled. "Sorry, honey, I've never been inside, I just know from what I've heard." He started to walk past, and I had to run to catch up.

"Well, maybe it's not like that anymore. I promise I won't stare." He shook his head and walked faster. Then the rain started, and as I tugged at his sleeve large damp blotches

4

began to appear on the gray suit. I shivered; the air, still close, moved over my skin and raised goose bumps. My father stopped, looking concerned.

"Just this once, please, oh, please," I wailed. "You never let me go, and you don't even know what's inside. Just this once, and I'll never ask again." I stood with my arms clutched across my middle, hunched over, looking pathetic. My father frowned and glanced around. The big tent was still closed; we had arrived early because my father had allowed time for getting lost. He took his coat off and draped it over my shoulders, then paused indecisively in front of the billboards advertising the sideshow, looking carefully at each one. The first poster showed a lady with the American flag displayed across her belly button. Next to her a snake charmer stood entwined with snakes the size of tree trunks. A sword swallower clenched his teeth around the jeweled hilt of a sword while smoke and flame issued from his mouth. A lady sat on a box with her ankles crossed under her chin, her knees pressed against her ears, and her hands draped down over her forehead like bangs.

I watched anxiously while my father's eyes went over each poster. The last was the one that really attracted me, a picture of a tiny man dressed in a tailcoat, held upright in the hand of a giant. I loved tiny things, and although I did not consciously believe in elves and fairies, in my passion for the miniature I wished that there were such things as tiny real people, small enough to sit on my hand. I was skeptical, but the poster suggested at least a possibility that my daydreams had some reality. Not to be allowed to see for myself was the worst deprivation I could think of. While I fidgeted with impatience my father continued to study the billboards, frowning thoughtfully. The rain thumped into the dust like so many minuscule explosions, and the air began to smell of wet clay.

At last he turned. "Well, Sara, this looks harmless enough. Just remember you can't believe everything you see." In a frenzy of excitement I hopped up and down beside him while he bought the tickets. Then we went under the steaming flap into the tent.

Inside, the space was broken up by larger versions of the posters outside, so that it was almost a maze. I craned my neck and stared into the dark. I heard the sound of feet shuffling through the coarse sawdust on the floor, the murmur of the crowd, and above this a strange bumping noise that in a moment I recognized as pipe-organ music, accompanied by men's voices speaking rhythmic unintelligible phrases. As we moved closer to a lighted platform, the noise resolved itself into a rapid singsong of words.

"Step right up, ladies and gentlemen, next party please, this way please." We moved along obediently, in time to the bumping music. The tent was quite dark inside, with brilliant slivers of light showing where the flaps parted slightly in the wind. In the beams of the spotlights that shone on the platform I could see the musty humid air moving, full of fine particles of dust, wood shavings, and smoke. The sawdust on the floor, dry when the first sightseers arrived, had been riled up into the air and into people's noses, so that the low murmur of voices was punctuated by sneezes and occasional coughs and throat-clearings. As more people moved in with their wet feet and trampled it down, the sawdust began to get gummy and smell sharply of resin. Clumps of it balled up under my shoes, and the damp scorched smell drifted up from the floor as our feet moved in it. The back of my nose began to feel sticky, but I sniffled the thick air as hard as I could, delighted, until the tickle made me sneeze.

"Oh, no, don't tell me you're getting another cold," my father said as he bent toward me with his handkerchief. "Here, blow." I buried my nose in his handkerchief and blew out some of the wood dust. Meticulously he folded back the dirty part and offered me a clean place. "Spit. You're all over cotton candy." He scrubbed my nose and chin with the damp handkerchief while I peered around his head for a glimpse of what was going on. Then my father straightened up and stuffed his handkerchief away while he looked around the tent. I handed him back his coat; I didn't need it anymore. He slung it over his shoulder, then took my hand.

We walked over to where heavy blue smoke hung in layers under the spotlights, and as I stood on tiptoe I could see a dark-faced man with a penciled moustache, wearing a turban, cautiously pulling out of his mouth a blackened sword. He held another sword flaming above his head, and as we watched he leaned very far back and plunged the burning sword down his throat. I felt a gagging sensation in my own, but even so I could see how he did it. When he leaned back, his throat and his chest and stomach made a straight line, and so presumably did whatever passage the sword went down. But didn't it burn? I tugged my father's shirt. He was standing with his arms folded over his coat, smiling. As I touched his arm he brought his hands up and clapped, laughing.

"Daddy?"

He turned to me, still smiling. "Yes, honey?"

"Why does the man do that?"

"Eat swords? Because it's an ancient Eastern custom to show how strong you are in withstanding pain. Like the men who sleep on beds of nails and walk on burning coals." I glanced back at the sword swallower, who was just now melodramatically gulping down both flaming swords at once. His throat worked, his Adam's apple bobbed convulsively, and his chest heaved. His face assumed a look of distracted agony. I clutched my father's arm; the man's throat and chest were no longer one smooth line. The crowd was very quiet, and the pipe organ rolled out a sound of drums.

"Won't he cut himself inside, Daddy?" I whispered. I was feeling a little sick.

My father leaned toward me slightly and put his arm around my shoulders. "Listen, Sara, remember what I told you about not believing everything you see? Well, as a matter of fact it doesn't hurt at all, because he's only pretending to swallow the sword. The sword folds up like a telescope in his mouth, so it only looks like he's swallowing it. It's what you call an illusion."

"What's that?"

"Something that looks a certain way but isn't." He hugged me and winked.

I looked back at the sword swallower, who was now grinning ferociously, standing next to a girl in transparent bloomers and a halter. Slowly they bent from the waist and then bounced up on their toes and danced behind the screen, holding the blackened swords like a bouquet. The swords still looked to me as though they were all one rigid piece, but I smiled complacently because I knew how it was done.

As we moved along with the crowd to the next booth, I pulled once more at my father's sleeve. "Daddy, when will we see the tiny man?"

He looked perplexed. "Tiny man?"

"Yes, the tiny real man in the giant's palm, he—"

"Oh, the midgets. Well, I'm sure they're around here somewhere."

The lights snapped on over another platform where a lady stood with her arms at her sides, doing what appeared to be absolutely nothing. She was dressed in brightly patterned tights that covered her from her neck to her ankles. As we came closer I could see an earnest-looking young man next to her pointing at various parts of her costume. As he pointed to the American flag stretched over her stomach it slowly began to wave, rippling back and forth like a real flag. My father tilted his head back and laughed along with the rest of the audience.

"Daddy, how does she do that?"

"The flag is drawn on her skin, honey, and when she moves the muscles underneath her skin, the drawing moves too."

"But why is she drawn on all over?" I could see now that she wasn't wearing tights at all, but a tiny bathing suit, and the rest of the patterns went all over her body, except her face, hands, and feet.

"Because she's the tattooed lady."

The tattooed lady turned her back to us, and the young

man pointed out a map of the United States drawn the long
way. Gracefully she leaned over sideways and rippled each
state as the young man named it. The audience gasped ap-
preciatively and clapped. As she turned around, I looked
closely at her and tried to trace out the patterns, following
some vines and flowers that twined down her legs. I had
gotten as far as her knees when suddenly two merry little
faces winked at me, one after another. They were her
kneecaps. I turned enviously to my father. "Oh, Daddy, can
I be tattooed like that someday, with faces on my knees?"

"I don't think you'd really want to do that."

"Why not?"

"For one thing, it doesn't come off, and if you change
your mind you're stuck with it. Besides, nice girls don't get
tattooed."

It had not occurred to me that the pictures did not come
off. I imagined someone, the earnest young man perhaps,
painstakingly drawing the designs with colored ballpoint
pens or greasepaint each morning, or at the least once a
week. "Doesn't it come off ever? Can't she wash it off?"

"No, honey, it's put right into her skin with a little electric
needle and colored ink."

I looked at him incredulously. "Doesn't it prick her
all over?"

"I'm sure it does."

All I could think of was my dentist and his needle. I shivered. "Why does she do it?"

My father rubbed my hair down over my eyes and began
to walk ahead. "So silly people like you and me will pay a
quarter to see her."

It simply could not be worth it. It seemed to me that my

notion of the ballpoint pens and daily drawing sessions made more sense. I yanked my father's sleeve and told him what I thought. He nodded slowly. "Yes, I suppose that's possible. Who wants to get pricked all over if you don't have to? But it would have to be indelible ink, right?"

We both smiled. Silently I made plans to try just a small face on my own kneecap when we got home. I took my father's hand and bounced on one foot. "Can we see the little man now, Daddy?"

My father looked around the tent. "I think we have to wait until it's his turn. The show runs in sequence, and we can't just move ahead." I stuck my lower lip out. "But there can't be too much more," he said.

We walked onto the next lighted booth, which contained a lady with a strangely shaped suitcase, out of which she pulled the longest snake I had ever seen. I watched, barely interested, while the snake wound sleepily around her. Next came a woman who tied herself in knots, then an enormously fat lady who bounced from one invisible foot to another in a wobbling jiggling dance, roaring with laughter. I was bored by these people and stood next to my father with my arms folded, entertaining myself by figuring out how all these acts could be illusions, as my father had said. Once or twice I consulted with him, but for the most part we stood side by side with our arms folded across our middles, passing the time, until finally a stage lit up in front of a poster picturing two tiny perfect people dressed in beautiful evening clothes. I shrieked with excitement and hopped up and down until I felt my father's restraining hand on my shoulder.

The pipe organ belched and a man came from behind the

backdrop with a black stick in his hand. I almost cried; he was regular-sized. "Daddy?" I wailed.

"Hush, Sara." I looked up at him, startled. He sounded annoyed. A small vertical line wavered between his eyebrows.

The man stepped forward and slapped his hand briskly with the stick. "And now, ladies and gentlemen, boys and girls, I have the actual pleasure of introducing to you the smallest man and woman in the world, Tim Tiny and his wife Trixie, only thirty-one and twenty-nine inches tall respectively, except for their size absolutely perfect in every way, actual tiny human beings!" He threw a hand out in the direction of the backdrop, and from behind it came two little figures. The man was dressed in a worn black suit with tails and a ruffled shirt. The woman wore a long gown of faded watery green satin, and feathers in her short hair. As they moved to the front of the stage I craned my neck to see better. They stood, not smiling, hand in hand. They were not what I expected, not the tiny perfect creatures my fantasies had conjured. They were not tiny; they were only little, not much smaller than I was. They certainly were far from perfect. Their heads were too big for their bodies; their faces were round and fat like a baby's, but puckered and wizened, so that they looked, standing there solemnly, like children who had grown old without growing up. Fat little fingers dangled from their pudgy wrists. Unlike me the female had breasts, but this made no difference to me. I was outraged.

"But Daddy," I shouted, "they're just children like me, only old!" Heads turned to stare at me, and the two dissipated moonfaces glared disdainfully down at me from the stage. Before my father had a chance to shush me the man on the stage started speaking, in such a jaunty tone I thought he must be glad I had exposed his game.

"On the contrary, little lady," he yelled, pointing the stick at me while I shriveled with embarrassment, "Mr. and Mrs. Tiny here are perfectly developed adult humans, aged thirty-two and twenty-six. Mrs. Tiny here"—he twitched the miniature fingers of the little woman—"has given birth to a perfectly normal, full-sized baby boy!" The crowd clapped politely, murmuring oh and ah to itself. Mrs. Tiny abruptly smiled an evil baby's smile, showing large yellowish teeth. The man talked on, twitching various parts of the little people's anatomy for emphasis, while I watched restlessly. I felt as though I might cry. Along with the embarrassment of being singled out and corrected, there was my disappointment. Years of nagging to be allowed to see the sideshow had ended in this colossal fraud. These were not the elegant beautiful small beings I had wanted to see, however remarkable they might seem to everyone else. I could see my father felt as I did; he stood with his arms folded, rocking slightly on his heels, his face expressionless as he studied the roof of the tent. Slowly the stiff feeling in my face receded and my cheeks cooled, and I began to feel merely bored instead of mortified.

Suddenly the man's voice stopped and a strange high-pitched noise took its place. The sinister babies' mouths had opened, and they were singing. I stood transfixed; they did not have grown-up voices, but they did not have children's voices either. Peculiar chirping sounds issued from their throats, sounding more than anything like a record played two speeds too fast. And that is probably just what it is, I thought in disgust. The midgets pirouetted, shuffled their little feet together, came into each other's arms with a lurch, and, grinning two malicious frozen yellowish grins, waltzed daintily behind the screen. The crowd clapped politely. I sneered and turned away.

But before we could move away the regular-sized man appeared again, swishing his pointer through the air. "And now, ladies and gentlemen, the other side of the coin, so to speak: our giant, Paul Bunyan Jones." A very tall man shuffled out from behind the screen, smiling fixedly, his eyes on some point far over our heads. "Eight feet six inches tall, folks, and only nineteen years old, still just a growing boy." The audience snickered.

"Daddy," I whispered as quietly as I could, not wanting to risk another onslaught from the stage, "he looks just like a great big man."

"That's right, Sara, he is just a great big man."

I took a deep breath. In my disappointment I felt compelled to make certain I knew the truth. "So there's no such thing as giants or fairies in real life, just big and little people."

My father bent close to me and stayed there, his arm around my shoulder. "That's right, honey. No elves or fairies or giants. Just people." It seemed to me that he frowned a little; perhaps he felt cheated too. I turned forlornly back to the stage.

The big man was still staring into the dark behind us, his huge hands dangling in front and slightly to the side, as if he wanted to show us that they matched. He was wearing a plaid flannel shirt, green work pants held high up on his chest by suspenders, and heavy boots like a lumberjack's.

The man with the pointer told us how each item the big man wore had to be specially made. Then he asked the so-called giant a question. Without changing expression the tall man opened his mouth and spoke. His voice was very deep and halting, like a record someone had put a finger on to slow down. It quavered uncontrollably, but all the time he was speaking he never stopped smiling. I fidgeted suspiciously. The midgets had been sharp and feverish; this man was so slow and deliberate he made me think of a mechanical dummy. Furious, I twitched my father's hand off my shoulder.

"Daddy," I demanded, "is *he* really real?"

"Yes." My father was putting on his coat. "Let's go." He reached for my hand and began to walk away.

"But we haven't seen everything," I wailed. Even though I felt defrauded, angry, and possibly even persecuted, I did not want to leave without seeing everything there was to see. I dug my Buster Browns into the sawdust and glared at my father's bow tie. "I'm not going."

"Haven't you seen enough? What else is there?"

In my mind I ticked off what we had seen and what there was still to see. I couldn't think of anything. Irritably I followed my father toward one of the slivers of light. Inside the tent, it seemed to be getting lighter; either the rain had cleared off, or my eyes had finally become accustomed to the dark. We were almost at the flap when out of the corner of my eye I saw another set of spotlights flash on. I turned. A large crowd—everyone but us, it seemed—had gathered in front of a booth set far back in the tent. The lights glared; around them the dark seemed very black. Beyond the crowd I could just see the head and shoulders of a beautiful golden-haired girl. She looked more like one of my fairytale pictures than anything else I had seen. A princess. A man stood next to her waving a stick. Of course. We had forgotten the magician. This had to be the magician and his beautiful assistant. The best was always saved for last. I tugged my father's coattail and ran back. When I got to the edge of the crowd I couldn't see over the people in front, so I shouted to my father as he came after me, "Lift me up! Lift me up!" I didn't care that he looked annoyed.

"Sara, we'll miss the circus if you don't come along."

"The magician, Daddy, I forgot there was a magician," I shouted, raising my arms. Sighing, he bent over and hoisted me up and around, piggyback. As my head went up, I saw the rest of the golden-haired girl. I clung to my father's shoulders, completely thunderstruck. For there was no rest of her to speak of. She was perched on the table, dressed in a flowered blouse fastened at the shoulder, and she had, as far as I could see, no arms or legs. Except for her beautiful face, in which her eyes moved back and forth over the audience, and her mouth, which twitched faintly as she licked her lower lip, she could have been my mother's dressmaking dummy, plunked down on a table wearing a half-finished dress.

I could feel my father's back and shoulders shifting under me as he moved to see, and then the characterless young man with the stick began to talk to us in a tone of earnest amazement. "Ladies and gentlemen, you see before you a little lady born without arms or legs, just as you see her here. Yet through her own efforts and strength of will she has learned to be self-sufficient, independent, and a useful member of society. She can type, write, dress herself, apply her own makeup, and answer the telephone." As he spoke the girl crumpled in the middle and with her teeth picked a long pencil out of a nearby jar. With one or two contortions of her mouth she adjusted it until she could clench it in her teeth and place the point on a piece of paper in front of her. She began with some effort to form large block capital letters.

Without warning my father swung me down from his back and turned toward the outside, yanking me behind him. I pulled back, enraged. This was the most fantastic thing I had ever seen. I began to tremble; my face got tight around the mouth and my throat closed up as if I were going to cry. I was being snatched away without reason from seeing the most incredible sight in the whole side-show, an exquisite wonder beyond my wildest dreams. Besides, I wanted to see how the trick was done. Defiantly I turned back to watch, folding my arms so my father couldn't pull on my hands to make me leave, and stood on tiptoe, ignoring him. If he wanted to take me away, he would have to drag me kicking and screaming. Then I felt his hand on my shoulder, tugging at me gently.

"No." I shrugged off his hand. Several people in front of us turned and shushed crossly. My father took his hand away.

As I watched transfixed through a space in the audience a small flesh-colored flipper poked out from the abbreviated sleeve on the girl's shoulder. The young man handed her a lipstick and held up a mirror. Turning her face into her shoulder like a sleeping bird, she painstakingly applied a coat of lipstick to her mouth, blurring it slightly. When she was finished she dropped the lipstick into the young man's

17

hand. She did not smile when the audience clapped approvingly, only blinked at the spotlights as though they hurt her eyes. The man put away the lipstick and placed in front of her a small flat typewriter with large keys. From under the hem of her dress two more appendages appeared and began to peck at the typewriter, one at a time. Each time she struck a letter she had to shift her torso. The audience gasped and clapped even more loudly. Behind me I thought I heard my father sniff.

"And now, ladies and gents, Linda the Armless Legless Torso will drink a glass of water!" The young man tucked a small glass of water into her neck, and she craned her face toward it, maneuvering her mouth onto the rim. Water sloshed and dribbled down her dress. With a small sucking sound she sipped at the edge. Suddenly my father reached from behind and, firmly taking hold of my hand, began to walk away. I could not see his face, only the line of his profile. I leaned back, about to protest. Without saying anything, without loosening the pressure on my hand, he turned his head and looked down at me. The crease between his eyebrows was sharp, the skin around his eyes looked strangely crumpled, and the rims of his eyes showed red even in the half-light. Bewildered, I straightened up and began to walk quietly beside him toward the tent opening. For a reason I could not guess, my father was upset and needed comforting. I tried to think of something to say to distract him. Remembering how he liked to explain puzzles and riddles, as we came into the daylight I turned to him and said brightly, "Daddy, how do they do that?"

"Do what, Sara?" He had stopped by the side of the tent and was wiping his face with his handkerchief.

"Make the girl have no arms and legs?"

He didn't answer, just squeezed my hand and kept wiping his face.

"Does she have no arms and legs really?" I persisted.

"Never mind, Sara. Let's get out of here." He looked around, then started to walk away. I ran to catch up.

"Daddy! How—"

"Oh, Sara, it's all done with mirrors. Now will you come on? We'll miss the parade."

I stopped dead. It was done with mirrors. My mind scampered back into the sideshow tent and all around the scene of the armless legless girl, placing mirrors here and there in my memory of it. I had not noticed mirrors at the time, but if my father said so they must be there. I couldn't really see how you could reflect away half a person's body without someone noticing the mirrors, but my father wouldn't have said so if it weren't true. I was still fiddling with the mirrors in my mind when I ran after Daddy into the big tent.

"I can't figure it out, Daddy. Where were the mirrors?"

He looked at me, his face without expression. After a time during which he seemed to study my face intently, he smiled. I knew that smile; it came most often after I had bombarded him with a long series of questions to which he patiently gave answers, until at last he smiled wearily. The smile meant, No more questions; the rest you do yourself. I groaned with disappointment, but then the noise of the circus parade distracted me, and I moved with my father to our seats in the big tent.

But when we drove home after the circus I remembered the puzzle and rearranged the imaginary mirrors again and again, trying to see how the girl's arms and legs could be reflected away. For a week or so after the circus I worked on the scene sporadically, with the hope that I might soon tell my father I knew how it was done. But I never got any further than the fact that the mirrors were there some-place. Sooner or later I might have asked my father for the solution, but less than a year after that he died unexpect-edly away from home, and I forgot the circus, the sideshow, and the armless legless girl and her mirrors for a long time.

Twenty-five years later I heard the phrase again, and what flashed into my mind was the picture of my father mopping his face as he turned away from the sideshow tent, his mouth pulled down, his eyes red. "It's all done with mir-rors." Trapped by his own innocence and badgered by my insistent curiosity and unwillingness to be fooled, my fa-ther had given the only answer he could think of to an eleven-year-old child who had just seen a real freak of na-ture. He knew that "it's all done with mirrors" did not ex-plain the armless legless girl, but the words distracted my attention from the horror and substituted puzzlement. I forgot the limbless torso and concentrated on the mirrors that had somehow achieved this miracle, and I did not think at all of what I had seen.

It wasn't until I heard the words again, as a grownup, that I realized there were no mirrors and never had been. Remembering that sideshow years later, it seemed to me I was no longer that little girl; instead I was my father, look-ing on first with amusement at the petty dishonesty yet ingenuity of the sideshow, then with pity and disgust and even fear at the powerlessness of human beings to prevent each other's suffering, the power even inadvertently to cause it. I felt shame too that I was not wise enough and firm enough to keep such sights from the eyes and mind of my little girl. My sense of impotence and guilt turned to bitter anger at those who exploit creatures like the golden-haired girl with darting frightened eyes, and I spoke, not to the anxious questioning face of my own daughter, but to the whole wretched spectacle of the sideshow and all it represented of the evil and grotesque in human life: "It's all done with mirrors."

My memory triggered by those words, I reexperienced the sideshow through my father, yet I never quite lost sight of the little girl, taking advantage of his easy nature, amazed and appalled by fantastic sights, yet loving him and believing him so implicitly that I took his ironic words, incredibly, as so much literal truth it saved us both. As my memory spins out the last frame of that sequence and the immediacy of the recollection fades, I wonder if my father would be disappointed to find that it took me twenty-five years to hear the words the way he actually meant them. And I wonder what my father would think if he knew that squalid little sideshow formed the background of my most complete and coherent memory of him, the only vision I have of him as he must have been seen by adults, not just my childish eyes, for irony is after all a tool used and understood almost exclusively by grown-ups.

But the fact that all this is wrung out of a single phrase in my memory makes me sometimes uncertain of the authenticity of my reconstruction. In the back of my mind always is the faint suspicion that I may have made it all up or transferred it from some movie I don't recall the rest of, out of my need to know my father as he was.

Yet sometimes I find myself in some absentminded daydream idly rearranging mirrors in a dusty tent amid the fraudulent cotton candy and shabby popcorn, so basically authoritative were my father's words. Dying young, he never shrunk to lifesize for me, and remains in the buried consciousness of my childhood the man who knew everything, who always spoke the truth.

A PLACE I'VE
NEVER BEEN

My father's hands are small and fine, but not a woman's hands. The nails are bitten short and ragged so that the skin at the tips of his fingers bulges over. The backs are freckled and tan, the palms and insides of the fingers rough and calloused, grit embedded in the patterns of whorls and lines. My father is a land manager for a big oil company, but he likes to make things, and when he is home from all the traveling he does, he spends a lot of time working on his latest projects. Last summer he built us a two-car garage from the ground up; now he is finishing the attic. He has turned part of the basement into a spare room for my grandmother when she visits. In another space next to his workbench is the unfinished layout for his electric train, and tucked around behind the furnace next to the washing machine is the theater he made for my marionettes. There is sawdust on the floor in little pyramid piles where it has fallen from the saw blade, except where it has been kicked aside and spread thin. The workbench is not messy; there is a place for everything, even if everything is not always in its place.

While my father is at home working in Toledo, the tools are everywhere. Sometimes when he is on the road my mother sneaks down, puts everything back, and sweeps up the sawdust, or I do, because it reminds me of him when he's away: the smell of the sawdust, the oil in the chassis of the small engine lying beside the curved HO-gauge track leading nowhere on its base of plywood, the prickly odor of horse glue and rubber cement, the metallic flavor of new nails. My father hardly ever works from a pattern or a plan; he'd rather make things up as he goes along. We ordered plans for the theater, but he and my mother altered them to make it collapsible so it fits in the back of my mother's car in case I ever want to take my marionettes on the road.

After my swimming lesson at the Y I meet my father at the office he uses when he works in town, and we walk up the street to where he parks the car. At the corner we stop at the tobacco store where my father buys his cigarettes. He stands in front of the cigar counter with one hand in his pocket, jingling the change that makes his right hand pocket a bulky lump. I stand beside him, pressing my forehead and hands against the pale blue neon strip along the edge of the counter, hearing the hum of the light, feeling a mild vibration through my skin. The man behind the counter bends down, changed to a gargoyle figure by the layers of glass as I watch him rummage around. When he stands up he is holding a stack of empty cigar boxes.

"Take as many as you want, Jim, they're free."

My father taps several of the boxes with the dime he is holding; they sound hollow, hard and wooden. He inclines his head toward me. "They're for my daughter here," he says, and winks at me. "Thanks, Art. Put it on my bill."

My father gathers up the cigar boxes, distributes them under each arm, and hands me a carton of Camels to carry. He leaves the store, walking swiftly, his hands shoved deep in his pockets, the cigar boxes clamped under his arms on either side, his coattails rumpled up and flapping behind him like the tail of some huge bird. I run after him, trying to catch up, wondering what I am going to do with six empty cigar boxes, but when we finally reach the car I am too out of breath to ask.

I watch as my father goes to work in the basement workshop. I must be quiet at these times, not ask too many questions, not distract him as he tries to work things out. His face is pursed as though he were about to blow a flute, and the two parallel furrows in his forehead I call his railroad tracks deepen as he squints and frowns at the pile of cigar boxes. Finally I can't stand it anymore.

"What are you going to make, Daddy?"

But he only grunts and mutters something I can't quite

25

hear. It may be "I don't know yet," or "You'll see," or "Don't ask." So often my curiosity gets the better of my patience, even though I have learned, in these years of sitting beside him on my high stool, waiting and watching, not to ask. My father is a lover of surprises, of mysteries and jokes and riddles, problems and complications that always seem to work out at the last moment. His favorite movies are thrillers, and he reads whodunits at night when he's at home. No matter what I ask him, he always knows the answer, knows how everything works and how to fix it, but he doesn't like to be asked what he is doing while he is doing it. Now he frowns silently, not in anger but in concentration, while I sit and watch and wait and see.

His hands move over the thin wood of the cigar boxes. He has scraped the labels off with a razor blade, and the curled-up pieces of paper lie in the little dunes of sawdust at his feet. Now he is drawing lines on the wood pieces, using a small ruler. When he puts the pencil down, the pieces of wood look like so many uncut puzzles.

"What are you two up to down there?" my mother calls from upstairs. I look up, startled, hoping she won't come down and interrupt us.

"Nothing much," my father calls. "Just a little something for Sara."

"Lunch in half an hour," my mother calls back. "Don't forget."

Nodding his head even though my mother can't see us, my father takes down a fine-toothed saw and begins to cut the puzzle pieces. It takes a while; the wood is brittle, the pieces narrow in places. But he is careful, and I am quiet. I sit with my back to the huge furnace, feeling fidgety, watching him as he lays down the cut-out pieces one by one as though setting up a game of solitaire. It makes no sense to me. After a while I lose interest, hop down and go wandering through the other parts of the basement, push the train along its track as far as it will go, wondering when my father will get back to that. I have promised him I will put together the cardboard model houses and stick up the little trees, but somehow we don't get around to it, what with one thing and another, golf on sunny days, a movie on rainy ones, me going to bed early during the week. There is the sound of light tapping from the workbench, but I'm not really paying attention, as I run my finger along the scrappy edges of the plywood country the train will run through one of these days, wondering if it resembles any of the places my father travels to.

"It's done," my father says.

I turn around. My father is holding a small chair no higher than eight inches with a back like a ladder and a solid seat, legs that curve down gracefully like our big dining-room chairs upstairs. I stare openmouthed; it is magic, a conjurer's trick, all those pieces dealt out flat like a deck of cards and now transformed into this. I don't know what to say.

"I'm going to make you another chair and a table to go with it," my father says. He holds it up, studies it, turning it in his hands, then gives it to me. "Careful," he says. "I don't think it's very strong. But now your puppets will have someplace to sit." He smiles at me. "Okay, kid," he says, "I guess it's time to eat."

So together we go up the stairs, me holding the chair carefully in both hands, careful not to crush it, my father with one hand resting lightly on my shoulder, the other jammed in his pocket, both of us laughing and talking, as though this time will go on forever and nothing ever has to change.

After school lets out in June I go with my father to the doctor. It's nothing serious; after all he is a young man, barely forty. Just now and then on the golf course, he tells the doctor, at the height of his swing, a pull, a tightness resisting, or at the top of a ladder reaching up to paint the eaves, a catch in the breath, a slight pain, a little dizziness; a time or two on the stairs walking up to his office, with me beside him, stopping, out of breath. Always before it has gone away, leaving him only momentarily ashen and trembling. I've gone with him because I need a physical for camp. He stays in the room watching while the doctor examines me, and I am embarrassed as I take off my shirt because my nipples are beginning to develop, little scorched marshmallow puffs on my flat chest, so I hunch over to hide them. "Sit up straight," he says sternly, and I do.

The doctor listens to my chest and feels my belly and looks in my ears and up my nose and down my throat and pronounces me fit for camp. Then it is my father's turn. "You wait in the waiting room," my father says to me.

"Why can't I stay?" I ask. "I want to stay and watch."

My father shakes his head, but he is smiling and I persist.

"You watched me," I say, my voice rising. "It's not fair. I want to stay."

"See you later," my father says firmly. He shrugs out of his suspenders and starts to unbutton his shirt.

"If you'll excuse us," the doctor says, taking my arm.

"It's not fair, I want to see," I protest, even as I'm being escorted to the door.

I look back over my shoulder at my father, who is sitting on the examining table, shirt off, his suspenders drooping down around his hips. "Go on," he says. "You're not missing anything."

I stand outside the closed door for a moment, hearing them chuckling together. What is the secret? I wonder, as I walk into the waiting room and sit down next to the fish tank, feeling cross. What are they trying to hide? But when my father comes out he is smiling. "Indigestion," he tells me. "You're fine too. Let's go." The doctor watches us from the doorway, round bland smiling face and blank glasses. Everything is fine.

The little kids are screaming and squealing, leaping around his feet at the bottom of the stairs, begging for one more piggyback ride upstairs. He shakes his head but finally gives in, hoists first my sister, Francie, then my brother, Vic, up on either hip. Their feet dangle down around his legs; they are getting big, six years old and almost five. Their hands clutch at his coat, his neck, his hair, whatever they can grab onto for safety. He lurches slightly, pretends he's going to drop them; they shriek with terror. He starts up the stairs with them, groaning, "You guys are much too big for this." When he comes back down his face is sweaty, and he looks pale. I stand by the front door with the big glass panel in it, hand him his overnight bag. Upstairs the kids call out, "'Bye, Daddy!"

"'Bye!" he calls to them. "'Bye, hon," he calls to my mother in the kitchen. "See you late tomorrow." He bends to kiss me. "See you later, Sari. You take care of everybody now." Then he hoists his new suitcase, goes out the door and down the steps. I don't watch him out of sight because I have things to do, and besides, he's only going to Sarnia, Ontario; he'll be back tomorrow night.

The sound of the phone ringing in my parents' bedroom wakes me up. It is just barely light; I look at the clock beside my bed. It is not the first time I have awakened this morning; I recall waking up and looking at the clock at four twenty, then turning over and going back to sleep. It is now 5 A.M., and the phone is ringing. Something terrible has happened. Suddenly afraid, even panicky, I jump out of bed and run to the doorway of my parents' room next door. My mother is sitting on the end of the bed in her nightgown, clutching the receiver to her ear. She is staring out the window at the gray light.

"At four twenty? . . . Yes, yes, I see. . . . No, not at all. I appreciate your calling." There is a long silence as she listens. I can't see her face, and I can't hear what the other person is saying, but I feel sick, because I know something has happened to my father, off on one of his trips. I lean against the doorjamb, and it creaks. My mother slowly turns to look at me. Her eyes are hollow-looking, her face slack and fallen.

"Daddy?"

My mother nods in slow motion, and I know he's dead. "Half an hour ago. Actually forty minutes," she corrects herself, looking at the clock. Her voice is as expressionless as her face. She blinks and jumps slightly as the phone jabbers in her ear. "What? Oh, yes, of course. Someone will come right away. As soon as possible." She pauses, listening, then says politely; "Thank you very much for calling." She replaces the phone carefully, turns her face back toward the window, folds her hands on her knees, and sits silently on the end of the bed, as if waiting for something. I remember my father sitting there on a day not long ago when the neighbors were having a big tree cut down two yards over. It was the tallest tree in the neighborhood, but we had one that was almost as tall and I was glad the tree was being cut down, so we would have the tallest. I said that to my father, and as he turned toward me, I was surprised to see the tears rolling down his face. I remember that now, watching my mother, thinking that only God can make a tree, and shouldn't somebody be crying about this? I shut my eyes, trying to picture my father's face and hear his voice, but already they are shadows, pale reflections in the window glass. I begin to sob and choke, one hand over my eyes, the other holding my stomach.

My mother is beside me, her hands on my shoulders, shaking me. "Sara, Sara, listen to me. You mustn't cry now. You'll wake the children. Please, Sara, stop."

I try to stop, but this only makes me cry harder. I put both hands up over my face.

"Sara," my mother whispers tensely, "If you have to cry, you can go next door. I'll call Mrs. Smith and you can go there. I don't want you to wake your sister and brother. I have to think. I must think what to do." She peers into my face, gripping my shoulders hard. "Do you want to go next door?"

I wipe my face with the sleeve of my pajama top. "No, I want to stay here. I'll stop, I promise." I sniffle and hiccup, but I am no longer crying.

"Go back to bed and try to rest while I think what to do. It's so early. We musn't wake the children; let them sleep. They'll know soon enough." She turns away, so calm.

I point to the other bed, my father's bed. "Can I stay with you?"

She sighs. "Of course." She reaches down, pulls back the covers. "Get in." She covers me up and tucks me in, then climbs back into her own bed, lies on her back staring at the ceiling, her arms over her head. She is thinking. I turn away and bury my face in the pillow, afraid I may start to cry again, start and never be able to stop. After a while I fall asleep again, and it is as though it never happened, or is happening all over again when I wake up, now, then, and always.

The rest of the day is confused. I hardly see my mother. Neighbors come and go, bringing food and taking away dirty laundry without a word, or with soft murmurings I can't quite make out. Someone picks up my little sister and brother, taking them away to play; someone else brings back clean laundry. My mother spends most of her time on the phone. I hear the words over and over again while I am down in the basement playing with my marionettes: "Jimmy died." The words sound strange to me; I had thought death was something you were, not something you did.

After lunch my best friend and her mother come to take me for a swim at their country club pool. Nancy and I stay at the pool while her mother goes off to play golf. It's crowded and the water is cold, but after a while I don't even notice how icy it seemed at first. I keep forgetting what is special about today, about me. But every so often a feeling of detachment comes over me, as if I were someone else watching me, and then it dawns on me. *Oh, yes, Daddy died.* The first few times this happens the realization gives me a funny feeling in the pit of my stomach, but pretty soon the words don't shock me anymore; it's as though I'm thinking about somebody else. Only once, as I'm swimming along underwater, holding my breath as long as I can, all of a sudden I stop. I hang suspended under the surface, floating quietly with my eyes closed. The water doesn't feel cold; I have gotten used to it and it is as though there is no water, no sensation, no noise except a slight hissing all around. I hang there relaxed, holding my breath, and I wonder if this is what it feels like to be dead. If it is, it's not so bad; I'm still me inside, in spite of the silence. Then I run out of breath, shake myself to the surface with a *whoosh,* and go right on laughing and talking and swimming. I am just the same; nothing has really changed.

It's not until we're driving home afterward that the thought occurs to me there must be some mistake. My father and I have always been so close—I have always spent more time with him than anyone else; my sister and brother are too little, and my mother is always busy with them—if he were really dead I would know, somehow, and feel different instead of just the same. By the time Nancy's mother drops me off at the house that afternoon, I am positive it isn't true. He can't have let this happen; I can't believe I'll never see him again. There has to be some mistake.

My grandmother and my mother's cousin Ralph have arrived from Skaneateles and are sitting on the porch with glasses of iced tea when I come up the steps. "Oh, my darling," my grandmother says, but I shake off her hand and go on up to my room. In a little while my mother comes up to tell me that she and Cousin Ralph are leaving the next morning for Ontario to "bring Daddy home." I don't say anything, but I am sure that once they get to the hospital, they will discover the mistake. It's not my father who has died, but some other man who looks a lot like him. They will get there and see immediately that this is the wrong person; knowing him well, they will see this. Between them they will straighten everything out and my father will come home, possibly sick, since otherwise he wouldn't be in the hospital in the first place, but still alive. I consider asking them if I can go too, but it's clear that my mother wants me to stay here and help Grammy with the children. So after they have left, I sit alone on the steps of our front porch, going over and over the whole problem in my mind. Inside the house my little sister and brother race around as though nothing has happened; I'm not even sure they've been told. My grandmother fusses and bustles through the house, gets dinner for the four of us, and we wait.

———

I am sitting on the steps when they come back that night.

"Hi, Sara," my mother says in a faint voice. "What are you doing up so late?"

She seems weary; otherwise there is no change, no relief. I wait for her to say something.

"We brought him home, honey. He's at Uncle Frank's."

I stare at her in disbelief. Uncle Frank is not really my uncle; he and his family live across the street. My first thought is that my father has been terribly disfigured and they don't want to shock us. He is waiting at Uncle Frank's house swathed in bandages, and we will go see him one by one, quietly so as not to disturb him. All of us together would be too much. Still, he will get better, and we can be together again. But then it occurs to me that she doesn't mean across the street at all. The Coyles are undertakers; it's the family business. What my mother means is that they have dropped him off at the Coyles' funeral parlor downtown. I stare at the two of them in consternation. They have not discovered the mistake. I'm the only one who can tell it's not my father. I should have gone with them, but it's too late now. I stand up.

"I want to see him."

My mother and Cousin Ralph stare up at me. My mother sighs. My grandmother has come out of the house and stands next to me. My mother looks at her, and my grandmother purses her lips and shakes her head. "Not a good idea, Martha."

"No, Sara," my mother says wearily. "I want you to remember him as he was."

"I want to see him," I repeat. I don't know what's going

on, and the only way I'm going to find out is to see whoever has been mistaken for my father.

"I don't want you to be upset," my mother says in the same weary tone.

"I promise I won't cry," I say quickly. My mother shakes her head, moves past me, Cousin Ralph holding her arm.

I follow them into the house and up the stairs, pleading, demanding, begging. I am twelve years old; I know what I am doing. They must let me see. Finally I wear them down, and they agree that I can go to the funeral home to view the so-called body before calling hours the next day. I'm so relieved; I'll know soon just by looking that it's not my father. I will calmly announce; "That's not him, you know." What happens after that I'm not sure. Since he hasn't come home when he said he would, he must have lost his memory and be wandering somewhere, not knowing who he's supposed to be, and we'll just have to go looking for him. But first I have to see.

The next morning I get dressed in a spotted shirtwaist, my best dress, the first one I've had on since school let out three weeks ago, and stockings and shoes with heels. I have to make sure my seams are straight, so I hold my mother's hand mirror over my shoulder and look at my reflection in the full-length mirror in the upstairs hall. But something goes wrong with the angle, and for a moment I can't see myself, only what looks like a hole in the mirror, or a tunnel into it. My stomach goes all cold and splintery as I look down the endless tunnel. *Why, that's eternity,* I think to myself as I stand there, *that's death.*

Horrified, I stare at it for a moment, but then I remember the time last summer when my father took me to the sideshow and we saw a girl with no arms or legs, or so it seemed, because when I asked my father afterward, he told me it was all done with mirrors. I have been puzzling over this off and on ever since, but looking in the mirror now and seeing myself reflected away, I have an idea of how it might work. Maybe that's it, I think to myself, maybe that's how he fooled my mother and the rest of them. Maybe it's not somebody else after all, but my father playing a joke, showing me how it's done. That's why it has to be me. I can hardly contain myself at this idea, and I'm too excited to eat much breakfast. It can be done, I think, and I'll know how when I get there.

I walk into the funeral parlor with my mother and Cousin Ralph, through a maze of little rooms and corridors opening out one after another, silently. Music is playing so softly I can't make out the tune, but it seems to come from everywhere. There is no other sound, not even from our footsteps on the carpet. No windows, just closed doors and corridors opening out of rooms, and soft light, soft music, and a faint hissing that reminds me of the swimming pool.

"Where is he?" I say and jump at the loudness of my own voice; everything is so muffled. Cousin Ralph points to a door at the end of the hallway, then takes my arm. I shake my head. "I want to go by myself." He looks at my mother. "I want to go by myself," I repeat. My mother nods; she and Cousin Ralph cross silently into another room where there are some chairs. I walk to the end of the hall and push open the door.

There are flowers all around, and the smell is so heavy it

surrounds me and seems to press me down. I'm feeling a little short of breath because it's as hot as a greenhouse in here. I look around and see another door. I walk over to it and push open it slightly to let some air in and some of the sickening flower smell out. Outside the air is bright and dry; I can see dust specks sparkling in the air, my vision is so clear. But over the rooftops of the buildings across the street the sky is the color of an old tin bucket; it looks as though it might storm. Close by the door a stunted tree is growing up through a dusty round hole in the sidewalk. Its leaves twitch randomly. I take a deep breath of the outside air, then turn around and walk back to look at the flower arrangements, thinking there might be mirrors hidden in them someplace. I bend my head and read the cards, following the semicircle of flowers around. There are flowers from friends, from relatives, from my class at school, but no mirrors, at least none that I can find. But then I remember I haven't even looked to see whether it's really my father or not. I look in the direction of the casket. From this angle, seen out of the corner of my eye, it's no more than an oblong shape on a raised platform, the lid propped up like a grand piano. I walk over and look straight at it.

The body certainly bears a strong resemblance to my father; I can see how someone might have made a mistake. A quilted satin blanket covers the legs and torso, but I can see that the body is dressed in my father's favorite suit, navy blue pinstripe, wearing his favorite tartan tie and blue shirt. Blue is his favorite color. Well, never mind, they can have the suit and tie; how were they to know it's all a trick?

I look more closely. The face is smiling, eyes shut, very peaceful looking. I don't feel the least bit upset; after all, this is our little joke, our secret. It's up to me to solve the puzzle. So I take inventory, starting at the top.

The hair is about the color of my father's, maybe a little grayer, wavy, but combed down flatter than he would have done. Two parallel lines not unlike the ones that crease my father's forehead—his railroad tracks—are just barely visible; in fact, all of the skin is smoother than my father's, paler in some places, rosier in others. All the other lines are gone. Why, he looks like he's been ironed, I think to myself, and have to cover my mouth to keep from laughing. Then I see there is a slight indentation across the bridge of the nose just where the garage door fell down on my father, smacking him right across the face, so he had a broken nose and two black eyes.

I stand back and fold my arms. The face is not unlike my father's, but I have never seen him so still, not even in sleep, so flattened out and smoothed. What bothers me most is the mouth; the lips look fake, too broad, false-looking, added on like the pink wax lips my friends and I sometimes buy for a joke at the dime store. I sigh and tap my foot, shift my weight in the unfamiliar high heels, look around the room wondering what to do next. Then out of the corner of my eye I see the chest rise and fall.

I move to the head of the casket and look back, staring at the chest. As I watch, it seems to move up and down, slowly but regularly. That's it then, I think, catching my breath and grinning to myself. He's alive. It is my father, creased nose, railroad tracks, pinstripe suit, and all, and he's alive. He was just pretending. No mistaken identity, no mirrors. All I have to do is let him know I know, and the joke will be over. I open my mouth to say his name, tell him I'm here and he can get up now. Meanwhile, my eyes are glued to the chest as it moves up and down ever so slightly.

"Daddy?" I say. He doesn't move, make any sign he's heard. Maybe he's gone to sleep, after waiting all this time? I reach out my hand to lay it on his chest.

And stop with my own hand held out, suspended over his chest, staring at his hands.

They are folded just below his chest, where the satin quilt stops. The fingers are loosely, even casually inter-laced, as though, reclining on a sofa, perhaps just waking up from a nap, he might be about to make some wry, slightly humorous remark prefaced by a wave. The backs are pale and almost transparent, flat and faintly lined, like wax paper someone has crumpled up and then tried to smooth out. The freckles stand out like flecks of paint. The nails are grayish white and very short, and though they are filed neatly straight across, not bitten ragged, the tips bulge over. The fingers are square at the tips; the hands are small and fine, but not a woman's hands. I would know them anywhere. These are my father's hands.

From where I stand, just at his shoulder, I can also see the backs of the fingers. They are oddly peaked and crum-pled, puckered as though they've been left in water too long. I stare at the shriveled fingers. They are not alive. The chest they are folded across is absolutely still. I seem to be looking at a flat, pale, smooth reflection of my father. The mirrors, I say to myself, it's the mirrors after all, and I look around wildly, inside the top of the casket, the ceiling, over my shoulder. There are mirrors everywhere, nowhere. And then the mirror tunnel curls up over my head like a wave, and the room starts to revolve around me. I see a little figure disappearing down the tunnel, and as I stand with my hand held out over his chest, over his folded dead hands, I know I have to touch him, it's the only way to know for sure if it's a trick; I have to touch him. I stand there with my hand held out, wanting to touch him, but I don't. I can't.

And then I am outside, clutching the stringy little tree with both my hands, pressing my forehead hard into its rough and wrinkled bark. And I am crying, loudly, hysterically, harder than I ever thought possible, all the time looking straight down at the little circle in the sidewalk at the tree's base, watching my tears fall and make crater after crater in the dust.

And Cousin Ralph is tugging at me, first gently, then almost angrily, pulling at me, wrenching my hands away from the tree, and shaking me. "Don't cry, Sara, it's all right, Sara, you mustn't cry like this. Sara. This isn't easy for any of us. Sara, you promised . . . you can't say we didn't warn you." He pulls me toward the door. I'm blinded by tears, but I resist. I won't go back. Cousin Ralph says in an exasperated voice, "Sara, I'm disappointed in you. What would your father say?"

"I don't care," I say between sobs. "I'm not going back in there."

We walk down the sidewalk along the outside of the funeral parlor. The walls are sandy brick and seem to rise out of the sidewalk as if they had always been there. I turn the corner and walk over to the car, get in the back seat, and wait while Cousin Ralph goes inside to find my mother. They don't look at me, just get into the front seat. No one talks. All the way home I stare out the side window, wondering how this could have happened. I have behaved badly, have failed everybody, especially my father. I should have gone after him, kept him from disappearing down the mirror tunnel. At least I could have touched him one last time to say goodbye, to let him know that I was there. To let me know that he was there, that he was really there.

On the way home it rains. The next day I refuse to go to the funeral, choosing to stay home with the babysitter instead, even though I am almost old enough to babysit myself. I've let him down; I should have known better, done better, at least been there when he died. But he's let me down too. He should have known better, if he was so smart, known enough to keep this from happening. I don't want to see him, not ever again; I'm haunted by the feeling that he's done this on purpose, left us for some obscure reason I'll never understand.

Later that summer when my mother wants to go back to the place where he died, to talk to his friends and the doctors, the hotel clerk, to find out all she can about his last moments, I refuse to go with her. Whatever his last moments were like, I don't want to know.

"It's better this way," my mother says in the flat colorless monotone of grief. She sits by the window, hands folded, in an attitude of acceptance, or is it resignation or despair? It is months, even years, before her voice loses this flatness, begins to assume the timbre of her violent mood swings, the racing speeded-up breathlessness of mania, the sloweddown growl of depression, so that years later I will remember her voice as a record playing always at the wrong speed, too fast or too slow. All this, her later breakdowns, will be perhaps the consequence of this death and other blows coming in quick succession, perhaps a weakness in her character itself, a flaw or crack into which tragedy seeps and freezes, expanding until it crumbles the facade. It is several years before I begin to hear the resentment, the blame, the stories of how he would not stop smoking, kept drinking too much, would not lose weight, wouldn't do the things the doctor told him that might have prolonged his life. He did not want to live that way. There is perhaps no other explanation. And it is many years more before she tells me that they knew all along he had a valve defect and could go any time, and that is what they lived with, this knowledge that he might die suddenly. She always expected it, that phone call in the night. She tells me these stories, and others at various times, but I try not to believe they are true, because I don't want to believe that he would choose to die in this irresponsible, uncaring fashion; that it is all his fault. It's no one's fault, not his, not mine. Still, it remains a mystery to me why there wasn't something someone could have done. If I had only been there, I find myself thinking at odd moments, surely I would have been able to do something to help.

"He would have hated being an invalid," my mother says in that passive, reasoned tone that passes for acceptance, even though she will never accept, will rail against this for the rest of her life. "It's better this way."

And I wonder in my childish literal way, not knowing yet

43

that it is what we all say when faced with an unacceptable occurrence that cannot be justified or altered, "Better
than what?"

After a summer of self-recriminations—how could I have
talked so mean to him so often, refused to go with him to
this place or that, smoked in the attic with my friend, not
eaten all the green beans on my plate, turning that one
rejected dinner into a showdown that lasted far into the
night, all the little things he minded and chided me for; I
could have been a better daughter if I'd known it was going
to be so short—gradually my grief lessens. I stop thinking
of myself as a special case requiring sympathy, about whom
teachers talk in hushed tones in the hallways. In the fall,
we suddenly pack up and move back to the place where my
mother grew up, to live with my widowed aunt and grandmother, leaving behind the house in Toledo with all his
improvements, the garage he built, the unfinished train
layout, and who knows what else. The puppet stuff goes
with me; in this one hobby I persist alone.

Years pass. I grow up, leave home. It seems I hardly miss
him anymore, seldom think of him, though once in a while,
walking down the street of some strange city, the thought
will cross my mind that I might meet him coming toward
me. After the first shock of recognition I will walk up to him
and say, "Where have you been all this time? What have
you been doing with yourself?" in a conversational tone,
because after all these years it would be pointless to accuse,
and besides, I'm glad to see him. But after a while I stop

talking to him in my mind, because the conversations get harder and harder to imagine. I get older and of course he stays the same, frozen forever in early middle age, his hair hardly gone gray. Only his hands can I imagine old, pale and withered as parsnips. I marry and have children of my own, try to imagine him a grandfather and can't. Neither can they, the boy and girl I sometimes in absentminded moments call by my little brother's and sister's names. They ask me about him sometimes, and I try to tell them, show them pictures, but it doesn't really help. I think sometimes about men I know who are his age, or the age he would be now, and try to match him up—he might have this one's silvery-white wavy hair, that one's cheerful disposition, another one's crochety businessman's political views. He cried when the tree was cut down but did everything he could to get into the army in World War II, raged in frustration, my mother says, when they wouldn't take him. Would he have minded Vietnam? Would he have been excited by the idea of men on the moon and stayed up all night to see the first moonwalk? Would we have agreed, or fought and grown apart?

But these are idle speculations. Most of the time when I think of him at all it is with muted sorrow that he has not been here to see how I've grown up, married a good man, had these beautiful and clever children, bought a nice house in Vermont; see how well I've done all these years without him. It would have been easier with him, but I try not to think about that. It's so long ago now, what's the point? Gone is gone, why search for fathers now? I've forgiven him for not being here, and I'm not even sure I'd want him to come back, even if he could. It's been so long; where would we begin?

That is what I say to myself, and I believe it. Yet for a long time after his death, I find myself looking for him in my dreams. Sometimes I see him walking toward me, hands always in his pockets, coat fanned out behind, smiling in sudden recognition, as if he didn't know he'd gone away and left me all these years. More often he's walking away, about to turn the corner, and I have to run after, because I'm the only one who knows him, knows who he used to be. Always in these dreams I find him walking down the street of a place I've never been before, and we pick up exactly where we left off all those years ago.

But after a while even the dreams stop, and he becomes no more than a faded recollection, flattened and smoothed, a smiling, insubstantial reflection somewhere in the back of my memory. I remember almost nothing specific about him, not his voice, his shape, the clothes he wore, the color of his hair. Only once, while I am watching my brother as he works away in a basement workshop he has made for himself, building furniture and making toys for his children, I see his hands and remember my father's hands making things for me, and I remark how small, yes, how very small and fine they are, improbably small for a man his size. I see my brother's hands and I think, Why, yes, that is the way they were, my father's hands, that is how they really looked. And I think, How odd, how could I forget? But I forget again. With so ethereal a memory I am safe from grief.

———

"Mom, Mom!" I hear my children crashing down the attic stairs this rainy day, excited by the latest treasure they've unearthed. "Look what we found in that box of old puppet junk! Whose is it? Can we have it?"

They stand there clutching it awkwardly between them, grabbing it back and forth with small grubby hands, looking up at me eagerly, neither one willing to let go. Where on earth has it come from after all these years? The other chair and the table my father made me are long gone. I can remember the last time I saw them, before the children were born, in a production of a Handel puppet opera I did with friends in graduate school. I never bothered to get them back afterward. Looking at David and Linnie now, jostling each other in excitement, yanking the chair between them, I am suddenly afraid they will wrench it apart, so I reach out and carefully disengage it from their hands.

"I'm sorry but you can't have it," I say. "It's mine."

They stare up at me, their mouths and hands gone slack, unable to believe this little toy chair is mine.

David, always the negotiator, recovers first. "Can't we even play with it? We'll be careful."

"Yeah," Linnie chimes in. "We'll be extra careful. Please?"

But I'm hardly listening to them as I dust it off, rub it a little, hold it in my hands, recalling the day my father made it for me out of a couple of old cigar boxes more than twenty-five years ago. It looks so fragile, but here it is, not lost, not even broken. And I find myself thinking of other things, suits and overcoats and snap-brim hats, the cigarette lighter that always fell out of his pocket when he bent over to pick me up, the fountain pen that leaked, the unfinished train layout, the tools, all long since sold, abandoned, left behind, lost or otherwise disposed of. I haven't even thought of it for years; still, here it is, with that arbitrary mindless persistence of objects. How can it be that this frail little object still exists and he does not?

And as I stand here holding it, suddenly it feels brand-new, and I am standing next to him, bewildered, while his hands move over the bits of cigar-box lid, conjuring this little chair. Small hands, fine but not a woman's hands, square at the tips, the skin bulging over, moving, always moving, never still. And holding the little chair so tight I almost crush it, afraid in this one instant to let go, I feel the chilling rush of time passing, leaving him behind, the frozen gap of years; I see that face gone deep in concentration, those shriveled hands so like my brother's hands, my children's hands, my own. . . .

And the children are clamoring, reaching upward, leaping around his feet, and he shakes his head but finally gives in, hoists first one and then the other onto his hips like saddlebags, their starfish hands clutching at his coat his neck his hair whatever they can grab onto for safety as I stand there watching, too old for piggybacks myself, stand there watching as he struggles up the stairs, lurching and grunting, pauses on the landing to give me a rueful look, then continues up. When he comes down I hand him his suitcase, stand on tiptoe to kiss him goodbye. "See you when I get back," he says breathlessly as he throws his coat over his shoulder, goes out the door, down the steps, turns to wave goodbye once more, but his face is ashen, and his skin is slicked with sweat. It is the face of a dead man. *Oh, God, I should have stopped him.* Come back! I call to him, but it's too late; he's already disappeared down the tunnel full of mirrors. I should have stopped him, but how could I have known?

Daddy, I would have saved you if I could. And here I am still running after, trying to catch you in that place I've never been.

FACING FRONT

The last time my brother visited us he left a reel of film for me, the 16 mm kind with no sound. "Something I found when I was cleaning out the attic at Mom's. I had a copy made for you." I just shrugged and put it on top of the refrigerator and left it for a while. It lay there, a big dark celluloid cookie, until I finally got around to borrowing a projector from the college and running it. We waited for the kids to go to sleep, and then I set up the projector on the coffee table while Phil unrolled the screen. I could tell the film wasn't very long, and it seemed like a lot of trouble to go to for six or seven minutes of somebody's old home movie, but I thought it might be amusing, even if it were only me waddling around in diapers squeezing mudworms through my fingers.

The big white square danced, glared, then was suddenly overtaken by the faded sepia interior of a room. The sunlight spiking through the windowpanes barely outlined the windows and woodwork, the folds of drapes like bleached carved stone, and I could just make out in the shadows on either side of the window two tall trumpet-shaped urns full of gladiolas. A wake? A christening? The only movement was the lurching and wheeling provided by the hand-held movie camera. The room bounced for a few seconds, then the image blurred into lateral streaks and we were transported outside and temporarily overpowered by the bright sunlight. "Take your finger off the button, dummy," I muttered, while Phil sat back with arms folded, repeating gleefully, "It's a classic, a real film classic."

Then suddenly, with no transition, there they were, and I knew we were watching my parents' wedding reception at my grandmother's house in Skaneateles, New York, July 31, 1938. They just burst onto the screen, my mother and father, swaying in front of the latticed area underneath my grandmother's wrap-around porch, arm in arm, with big grins on their faces, my mother all dark lines and angles, black hair and eyebrows and vivid dark lips and eyes, my father blond and slim, shiny-faced and curly-haired, both proud and confident, innocent of any suspicions about their future. The breeze blew my mother's veil across her face and my father said something out of the corner of his mouth, and my mother smiled even harder, put up her hand to hold down her veil, then looked up at my father and excitedly jiggled his arm with her other hand, which he pressed closer to his side. My mother hung on his arm and beamed, two large dimples shadowing her smile. The person with the camera must have said something about kiss the bride, because my father appeared startled and shook his head, and my mother lowered her eyelids and looked demure, and then they bent toward each other and briefly touched lips. Then they came to attention, eyes front, like two mechanical soldier dolls, and my father snapped a mock salute. They laughed and sidled away through the shrubbery, and the camera panned around to the guests; all my aunts and uncles, my father's father, the minister, his wife, my chubby grandmother with the plain frontier schoolmarm's face, wire-rimmed glasses and all, and my other grandmother, my mother's mother, stout, elegant, faded, with white hair and pale thin mouth, looking exhausted but relieved.

The whole scene had that jerky, slightly jived-up tempo of old movies, but there was something else wrong. Nobody looked quite the way I remembered them; nothing matched the pictures I had filed away in my memory. Even my grandmother's house with the high latticed porch was oddly unfamiliar.

"There's something wrong," I said. "Something's not right about the faces."

"I don't see anything wrong," Phil said. "I'd know your mother anywhere; she looked as crazy as a coot even then. It's that wild, glassed-in look in her eyes."

"It all looks strange, not the way I remember it."

"Maybe you don't remember it right because you weren't born yet."

"I don't think that's it. But never mind. Let's just watch."

We watched for a few more minutes while the camera nosed around the grounds of my grandmother's house, trying to keep up with my parents as they mingled with the guests. Then the film hiccuped and my parents came out of the front door dressed in street clothes and started down the steps, while the guests awkwardly hurled rice at them and they bobbed and ducked, laughing. My father got a handful in the eye at close range from my mother's sister Rozzie and stopped to wipe the rice away like so many hard little tears. They hurried over to a car parked in the street alongside the house, got in, and drove away. The film ran on rather aimlessly, forlornly, back over the wedding guests, the house, the goldfish pond, until the last frame jerked away and the film slapped around the take-up reel.

"Why did your father have an English car?" Phil asked.

"Huh?"

"The car. The steering wheel was on the right-hand side."

The white screen flooded our eyes and I flicked off the projector lights, letting the machine cool down. I thought about the steering wheel. Then I stopped the take-up reel. But this time I turned the film over, reversed it, because I thought I knew what had happened. Whoever had copied the film had rewound it inside out. My brother hadn't noticed anything wrong because he didn't know the faces of most of the people or remember my grandmother's house. It gave me a chill to think that of all the people who might ever see this movie, only I would see that all the faces in it were oddly reversed, mirror images of what they ought to be. The car alone wasn't a certain tip-off; my father might have driven a British car. Even the people in it wouldn't know, if they were still alive, which most of them weren't, because they would be used to seeing themselves that way, the way they looked in the mirror. It wouldn't occur to them that they were supposed to be seeing themselves as others saw them, and they would never miss the mild shock of nonrecognition that comes with seeing all your moles and droops and quirky asymmetries in their proper places. I felt oddly excited as I waited for the film to rewind. When I started the projector again, I could see from the very beginning that everything was all right. The sepia sun-streaked room decked out with gladiolas was my grandmother's parlor where the wedding ceremony had taken place, and the slope on which the house was built ran downhill the way it always had. The faces were familiar. I sighed and settled back to watch the film again, no longer puzzled by the strangeness of it all.

At last my parents stood poised at the top of the stairs once more; then they were at the bottom, arm in arm. After one last laughing look, they turned away from the camera and walked across the lawn toward the car. I watched their young, jaunty, straight-shouldered backs as they walked away; suddenly they seemed so vulnerable, their happiness so fleeting, and I felt like a mother watching her two children walk away, hand in hand, into the woods alone. Then I saw that the back of my mother's dress was undone at the top, so that a small patch of white skin showed. No one else seemed to notice; nobody rushed over to do it up. My father helped her into the car and then walked around and got in himself. The two of them smiled and waved, my father leaning across my mother, and then they drove away.

Twenty years later my mother ran down those same steps, leaving behind three bewildered, underage children and the contents of every drawer, cupboard, closet, rubbish can, cereal box, flour bin, and paint tin dumped out and mixed together on the floor. She had gone for three days without sleep, chattering to herself nonstop, playing jazz records at top volume on the stereo. I was seventeen, my sister eleven, and my brother not even ten yet. Worried and then frightened, on the third day I finally called the family doctor and then the police. My mother saw the police car pull up alongside the house near the back; she ran out the front door, down the steps, across the lawn, and into the fields behind a neighbor's house without looking back. The police caught her about a mile away and brought her back to the house to say goodbye to us before they took her to the state hospital. She looked at me, still all dark lines and angles, and her eyes glittered like a lathered racehorse's; she looked very happy, even triumphant. Her cheeks were flushed and her breathing shallow. She reared her head back and stared at me with her proud, satisfied, crazy eyes, and said, panting, "Did you call the police?" I nodded. "I could kill you for that," she said. The tall policeman holding her arm blinked, stared at her, at me. "But I won't. Maybe now I can get a little help around here. Get the picture?" And she turned away. The second policeman grabbed hold of her other arm, and the three of them marched out of the house and down the steps to the waiting police car. She was forty-four, and my father had been dead almost exactly five years.

II

My mother always claimed the beads were solid gold, that Uncle George, my father's uncle, had bought them in

France for her, and they were very valuable. The jeweler who restrung them for me said they were gold-filled and very nice, but not of any great value. My mother wanted me to have them and pass them on to Linnie, she said, as she handed them over to me two summers ago at the bottom of the stairs in the house in Skaneateles. She had gained weight in the last ten years, less running around, she thought, or possibly it was the lithium that made her so logy, but anyway the choker had gotten too small for her neck, and she wanted me to have it. I put the beads around my neck, reached back, and fastened the clasp. It was a choker, all right. I gagged, not liking the feel of cold metal so close around my throat. I pulled on it slightly and the chain gave, scattering the beads on the floor. My mother and I went down on our hands and knees. "Oh, dear," my mother said. "I wish you hadn't done that. But never mind. We'll find them. They needed restringing anyway." We groped around in the dust at the bottom of the stairs, found the beads in cracks, next to the wall, under the rug, and collected them. I put them in a plastic bag, took them home to Vermont with me, and had them restrung. There must have been one or two beads missing, because when I picked them up and tried them on, they were even tighter than before. The next time I talked to my mother on the phone I told her. "Oh, never mind," she said. "Just have the jeweler put a guard chain at the back, and you can wear them undone."

"But it will look funny," I said.

"But it's the back of your neck. Nobody ever looks at the back of your neck. It'll be all right; you'll see."

As I put the beads away in my jewel box I thought about

what my mother had said, and about all the years I'd lived with her, the hours I'd spent, the letters I'd written, the phone calls I'd made, trying to make some connection, trying to get her to face up to herself and her life as it really was. My father had been dead since 1953; more than twenty-five years later she still mourned him, bitterly resented the thought that he had carelessly abandoned her to this life alone. She wouldn't give him up, and though his image wavered and changed from hero to villain and back again, it remained always at the back of her mind; he was her final audience. Of course she couldn't turn around and look behind her, because that meant facing up to what she had lost.

So often while growing up I would see her walk out of the house with her hair flattened and matted at the back, her dress unzipped at the top, the hem falling down or her slip showing, her stocking seams as crooked as a hurrying snake. She would turn and smile at me, implying the question How do I look?, and I never told her she wasn't finished behind, not after the first time, when she gave me a look of haughty disbelief, fluffed her dress in front, and stormed out of the house, insulted. The facade of her life must have seemed plausible enough to her as she skimmed past it, resisting my attempts to make her look around and see its incompleteness: the flat walls propped up with angle irons and toothpicks, sandbagged into place, the doors leading into rooms that did not exist, and stairs dropping off into empty space. And there we were, my sister and brother and I, trying to pick our way through the debris.

The other day I made my daughter a grilled cheese sandwich and charred it on one side because I was paying attention to something else. Without thinking I flipped the sandwich over burned side down and served it to Linnie, who took one bite and looked at me with an expression of outraged betrayal, then disgustedly spat the soggy mess onto her plate. As I threw the sandwich in the garbage I recalled all the grilled cheese sandwiches and slices of toast and pancakes my mother had served me in my life, burned side down. What an injustice it is to be served a sandwich burned side down, and not to realize it until you've already bitten in. There you sit, small and humiliated, knowing that sooner or later you'll either have to choke it down or spit it out.

III

When my father died suddenly of a heart attack away from home, my mother was at first stunned into silence. She hardly spoke in the daytime. But I could wake at any hour of the night and hear her murmuring and crying in the dark. If I went to her room and asked her if there was anything I could do, she would just say, "I'm not crying." Sometimes I would sit on her bed and try to comfort her just by being there, but the next night it would be the same thing, the precise mechanical sobs going on monotonously, even involuntarily, and after a while I gave up. Finally near the end of the summer she went to a psychiatrist, who arranged a few shock treatments for her depression. But she didn't have to go away anywhere, and in fact she did not seem very different to me, just sadder, and life went on pretty much the same until one day in November my Aunt Rozzie arrived, called a moving van, packed us all up, and moved the four of us from our house in Toledo, Ohio, back into my grandmother's house in Skaneateles, where my mother and father had been married fifteen and a half years before.

Six years pass. I'm eighteen. My aunt and grandmother, with whom we've lived all this time, have both died of cancer within a year of one another, leaving my mother the sole survivor of her immediate family and owner of the house on State Street. Since her breakdown the summer before, things have been relatively calm. Back from the state hospital nearly a month, my mother now sleeps in what was my grandmother's room. From my room next door, I hear again the crying in the night. I try to be enlightened about my mother's depression; she has so much to grieve for. It's summer, and the birds are chirping outside the window. In the fall I'm going seven hundred miles away, to a college I chose partly because it was so far from home.

My mother has not gotten out of bed for three days. I have already asked her several times if she feels all right, but she doesn't answer, just lies there facing me, her eyes closed. Her eyelids flutter, pale and transparent as a moth's wing. She looks relaxed, as though she is sleeping, but she isn't. Once in a while her eyes open and she blinks, then huddles farther into the blankets. I've been getting the meals and taking the children out in the afternoon to the lake, where we swim. I leave my mother alone most of the time; maybe she needs the rest. But finally on the fourth day I go upstairs and stand in the doorway of her room.

"Can I get you something to eat?"

"No, thank you."

"Are you all right?"

"No."

"Are you sick?"

"No."

"Then what's wrong?" I feel impatient, irritated. If she's not sick, why doesn't she get up?

Her eyelids flutter but do not open. A tear oozes out of one corner, hesitates, coasts jerkily around the dark hollow under her right eye, then drops onto the pillow. "Oh, Sara," she whispers, so faintly it's little more than a sigh. "I hear the birds outside the window, and they're saying *Stu-pid, stu-pid, stu-pid.*" As if to answer her a bird chirps up, as clear as water, and I hear it say *phoe-be, phoe-be, phoe-be.* The tears roll out from behind my mother's eyelids, but she doesn't make another sound.

I call the doctor, who tells me there's not much he can do, but finally we convince my mother to commit herself to the mental hospital again for a few days. She stays two weeks. When she comes out, she seems much happier, and there's no more question of the birds telling her she is stupid. I'm relieved, because it means I'll still be able to go to college in the fall. Meanwhile there's no more crying in the night.

IV

We come down Route 20 in Skaneateles, Phil and I, past the small Gothic-style church where we were married in 1964, past the park at the head of the lake. We've made this trip quite a few times in the five years we've been married; it's not that long a drive from Vermont, where we both now

61

teach college. The lake is, as always, translucent, breath-taking, inexplicably blue. We turn right and start up the hill, passing the white houses with dark shutters stacked one after another in stately progression, their lawns trimmed, the large trees stooping protectively over the street. When I was growing up, these houses were mostly inhabited by little old ladies, many of whom were distantly and complexly related to my mother. Now there is the odd tricycle, the wading pool, but the street is still very quiet, very stately. My heart is fluttering. We haven't seen my mother in over a year, since she came back from a brief sojourn in Massachusetts. We haven't told her we're coming, because just once I'd like to catch her when she's normal, show Phil what she's really like.

Phil looks from side to side at all the beautiful houses. "This place is incredible. What must it have been like to grow up here?"

"I remember it was boring in the summer. And lots of little old ladies. The same thing day after day, going to the country club to swim, a little golf, a little sailing . . . you know, the usual."

"But then yours is an unusual case, I suppose."

"Not necessarily. It's a genre. Upstate Gothic. Idiots in the attic, skeletons in the closet, Uncle Hubert's drinking problem, Aunt Bertha's secret drug addiction. . . ."

"We're here." Phil turns the car into the drive, bumps up onto the two parallel concrete runners that lead to the garage, the latest thing for families with motorcars in 1926. They're a little broken down at the edges now.

The truth is, I'm anxious. Since we've been married, Phil has seen most of what my mother has to offer, but it's still unsettling, to me if not to him, never to know what you're going to find when you open the door. These many years I've learned to read between the lines of letters and behind the tone of voice on the telephone, to surmise where my mother is in her wayward cycle of highs and lows, but the pattern has a disconcerting way of turning back on itself, shortening up, so that where you might expect there would be time left in the normal range, say a month or more, suddenly she's off again. Once I returned from college unexpectedly, thinking I might catch her when she had leveled out and have a little talk because all the signals were good, walked in, and found the contents of a three-story Auburn pawnshop spread around the house, on the floor, in the chairs, little figurines and brass objects, watches, golf clubs impishly stuffed into corners and under cushions. But never mind. The trick is, my sister says, not to let her know you're coming, because if she knows, she fidgets.

The kitchen door isn't locked; I push it open, sniffing. Sometimes the smell of the place is a clue. Even an instant's forewarning is better than none, but what do I expect? My mother to pop out of a can like those wiggly fabric-covered springy snakes they sell in novelty shops? I tiptoe in, feeling like a spy.

"Why are we doing this?" Phil asks from behind me.

"I'm just checking. I want to see how she is."

"You know how she is. Impossible. Let's get out of here."

His message is, and has been for some time, Give up. But I won't, not yet. "I can't," I answer. "She's my mother. I love her; I'm responsible for her." But even as I say it, I wonder if it's still true.

Phil says noncommittally, "Hmm." He thinks the whole thing is a bad idea.

The sunlight streams into the kitchen from the dining-room windows beyond. Things look normal. It's very quiet. In the sunbeams float minute particles of dust, stratifying the rays so they slant to the floor like beams from a row of spotlights. We make our way across the kitchen. Briefly I wonder how it would be to enter unannounced and still know what to expect. But I'm suspicious now, even more than suspicious, jumpy. There is something distracted about the place, in the air, in the silence. There is no food to be seen, not on the counters, in the sink, or on the stove, no dirty dishes. Then far away I hear the sound of something being abraded, an exhausted sawing noise.

"Come on," I say to Phil, who is backing away toward the door.

We find the first hole in the living room, in the chimney wall. The plaster has been chipped away, exposing the bricks for an area of about a foot square. There are several other holes in other walls, and in one place the plaster has been chipped away from the lath and the lath broken through to expose the space between the beams. I poke my head inside; there's nothing to be seen but a pile of broken lath and powdered plaster. It's like looking at old bones. There is the sound of hammering upstairs now, and the sawing has stopped. I walk down the hall into the parlor where my parents were married. The books have been turned out of the shelves into piles on the floor, and there are holes ranging from fist to tray size in the walls between the shelves. In the false wall in front of the old fireplace is a hole almost big enough to step through.

"What the hell is this?" Phil murmurs. His voice is awed, respectful, as though he were in a museum contemplating something wonderful. "Is she in there?" He peers into the hole in the false wall. "Nope."

But I know where she is. I walk to the bottom of the stairs and look up. She's standing at the top, silhouetted in the dim light, outlined by the white plaster dust that powders her hair, her eyebrows, her shoulders, the folds of her dress. Are her eyes glittering, or is it just a trick of the light and my expectation, knowing that the look must be there, knowing what she's done, what crazy, frantic energy it must have taken to punch and tear these holes?

"Hi, Mom," I say to the figure at the top of the stairs.

"Who is that?"

"It's Sara."

"Oh, Sara!" She sounds enthusiastic, breathless. "I'm so glad you're here." She comes quickly down the stairs, making no attempt to brush the dust from her face and her clothes. Under the white film her skin is flushed. She walks past me, then turns and faces me and smiles. Her eyes are wild, evasive. They have a secret.

"I'm having the most wonderful time," she begins. But the rest of the sentence is lost. She falters, looks confused. "I've been looking for . . ." She pauses again.

"I can see that." I try to sound neutral, understanding, but it doesn't work. Her expression changes from triumphant, victorious, radiant, to that of a guilty child caught startled in the act of dismantling an expensive and forbidden but fascinating belonging of her parents.

"But I can't . . . I haven't . . . it must be here somewhere. I just wanted to see."

"What is it?"

She stands silently, staring at me, and the guilty look dissolves into that opaque but crafty look I've seen in the glass eyes of stuffed wild animals. She's pulled the blinds down behind her eyes. She smiles and dimples her cheeks so that some of the plaster dust flakes off.

"I'll never tell."

I turn around and walk out.

As we're driving home Phil finally says, "Well?"

I feel like crying, but I don't. "I feel so sorry for her," I say. "She seems so desperate, looking for something, who knows what. . . ."

"Desperate, hell. I thought she was having the time of her life."

"Maybe so. It's so hard to tell."

"Remember what the doctor said. Let her step in her own shit."

"Is that what the doctor said?"

"Or words to that effect."

"Oh. Words to that effect."

"Well, it's easier, isn't it? And she's survived so far. Let her have a good time. She's not hurting anybody."

"Right."

"Let's just not visit, okay?"

"Sure."

"Don't take it so hard." He reaches over and squeezes my hand. His fingers are warm.

"You don't understand. She's my mother."

"No, I'm sure I don't. But you can carry that sort of thing too far, you know."

"Thanks. I'll keep it in mind."

Phil grips my hand harder. I feel like a balloon full of hot air, straining to take off, and his hand is the rope that holds me down to earth. I hold on to his fingers. We drive in silence for a while. Before long we'll have to start looking for a place to spend the night. Phil's voice breaks in, splitting the dark. "Still," he says, "you can't help wondering what she thought she'd find behind those walls. What was she looking for?"

"Some sort of breakthrough."

"Is that a joke?"

"Not necessarily."

V

The telephone rings, dribbling into my half-asleep consciousness with the persistence of a leaky tap. It's too late to be good news. I grab the phone, hoping it won't wake up the children.

"Hello?"

"Hello, Sara?" It's my sister, calling long distance. Her voice is tense, slightly hollow, as though she were speaking from inside a tin can.

"Yeah, hi, Fran. What's wrong?"

"She's off again. Way off."

I sigh, sit up, shove the phone tighter into my ear. My fingers hurt, I'm gripping the receiver so hard.

"Up or down, and how bad is it?"

"She was high, but she got in trouble with the police because she was weaving her car all over the road—she thinks the FBI is after her—and they thought she was drunk driving. But then after she gave them this story about being an ex-FBI agent and the FBI wouldn't let her quit and was out to get her, the cops took her to the state hospital. One of the clowns there stuffed her full of heavy-duty tranquilizers and then discharged her. She took them for a week and then crashed. She's down, really down. I stopped by the house and she's just sitting in a chair, staring at the wall. She must have tried to feed herself a couple of days ago and couldn't do it. There's a can of soup still stuck up there in the opener. It's gone bad. Chicken noodle."

"What do you want me to do?" I feel panicky already; the baby's only a few months old, and David's just three. I can't go anywhere.

"Well, nothing. I just thought you ought to know. I'm going to have her readmitted."

I sigh, switch the phone to the other ear, and wiggle my petrified fingers. This is the fifth time in the last four years, since the day she poked all the holes in the walls of my grandmother's house. At least Fran has taken over. But how long can she go on? Tentatively, speculatively, I say to my sister, "Don't you ever wish she'd die? She's so miserable anyway, and then there wouldn't be any more of this. It would be all over."

There's a silence on the other end. Have I shocked her? She's a lot younger than I am. But her voice is matter-of-fact when she finally answers me, as though she's been thinking about it.

"I know how you feel, or I'm beginning to. But Sari, she is our mother, you know. Always and forever our mother. Even if she is crazy."

"I know. Sometimes I just don't care anymore. I'm tired

of it. Up down turn around, and it's been going on for as long as I can remember. The doctors don't do anything that works, and she's just miserable. It's no way to live."

"How do you know?"

"Aren't depressed people miserable by definition?"

"I don't know. There are always the highs."

"The highs are lower than the lows. How many more years of this can you take?"

"Oh, I don't know. You did ten, I'll do ten, and Vic can do ten. How many's that?"

"Not enough."

"Then we start over. You do ten . . ."

"Leave her."

"What?"

"Leave her. Don't have her readmitted. Just let her stare into space for as long as she wants. Who knows what she sees? Maybe she'll come out of it by herself."

"Yeah, and maybe she won't. You haven't seen her. She can't do anything. She'll die."

"That might be the best thing that ever happened to her."

"You don't mean that."

"Of course I do. But you do whatever you think is right. It's your turn."

"God, you're callous."

"I'm not callous. I just happen to believe that people ought to be responsible for the consequences of their own actions. Let her step in her own shit."

"I don't believe you, I really don't." There's a long silence. The phone sounds hollow. "Goodbye," Fran says abruptly, catching me off guard.

"Good luck," I shout, but my sister has hung up before

the words go down. It's several days before I hear from her. The phone rings in the daylight.

"Hello. Sara?" My sister's voice sounds tired, wrung out.

"Yes?"

"It's all over."

The words rush against the tension in my chest like so many small birds flying headlong into glass. I'm impenetrable. For a long moment I don't know what my sister means, and I don't want to ask.

"Sari? Are you still there? Did you hear me? Everything's taken care of. Mom's all set. There's a new doctor who's got her on lithium, and he's pretty sure it's going to work. Our troubles are over. I thought you'd like to know."

VI

My mother seldom calls now, but letters come frequently, and it's been long enough since the last episode of craziness that I don't even bother to scan her handwriting for signs of imminent breakup, the way I used to listen for those stomach-walloping clues of tone and catch phrase in her voice over the phone. We're all feeling pretty secure. As long as she takes it, the lithium works for her, smooths over the hills and valleys, and at the age of sixty-two my mother has subsided into a reasonable facsimile of an elderly, respectable widow lady who sits sedately underneath her white hair and knits sweaters and mittens for the kids.

When the letter comes it looks just like any other letter. There's nothing erratic or thready about the handwriting on the envelope, and no wild postscripts wandering around the margins, snaking back through the place and date to end in a barrage of exclamation points. This time there's just the place and date—Auburn Memorial Hospital, September 13, 1976—and "Dear Sara: I'm lying here recuperating from my mastectomy and feeling pretty good. . . ."

The phone rings and it's my sister. "Did you just get a letter?" she asks.

"I sure did."

"Could it be true?"

"I don't know. It doesn't strike me as the sort of thing you'd have for a delusion, given a choice." Silence. We're both thinking about what this means.

"Well, what do you think?" Fran finally says.

"She didn't tell us a thing, just went and took care of it all herself."

"'Didn't want to worry you,' she says. It's not like her."

"I know. Have you talked to Vic?"

"Not yet. But he'll check in later."

"You know what this means, don't you?" my sister says.

"What?"

"It's one more goddamn thing we can inherit."

"I don't get it."

"Like being a manic-depressive. You inherit the tendency for this, too. Just one more goddamn burden she's unloaded on us." My sister sounds disgusted; she's still getting over her last siege two years ago, in 1974, when my mother, having taken herself off lithium, wrecked an entire hotel room and assaulted the policeman who came to get her. Fran told me it took four men to get her into the police car. That's when Fran gave up and moved to Colorado. Now everything has to be done long distance. I try to concentrate on the problem at hand.

"Well, I think we ought to consider what it's going to do to her head once the shock's worn off. I think I'll call her up and tell her I'm driving down."

"Right. You're closer."

"Sure enough, I'm closer. Okay. Thanks for calling. See you."

After I hang up the phone I try to piece together the story from my mother's letter. But there isn't enough to go on. She sounds so normal and in control; there's got to be something wrong. So I call her up at Auburn Memorial, and she's not even in the hospital anymore, she's gone home. I call her at home. She answers after a few rings, sounding breathless.

"Hello, Mom. How are you?"

"Fine, did you get my letter?" She sounds eager, as though she were ready with a piece of extra good news.

"Yes, I'm driving down."

"Oh, no. Don't be silly, you were just here a few months ago. I'm fine, just a little stiff, and the incision pulls when I breathe but there's nothing to it. Really."

"Phil can stay with the kids and I can be there by to-morrow."

"No." her voice is emphatic, risen slightly in pitch. I wait for the breakdown. It doesn't come. "I don't want you to come all this way. I'm all right. Really. I can take care of myself. Don't worry about me."

The question is, what to say next. All these years of bizarre phone calls, dotty letters with clues in code saying "Come and get me, I'm gone again," driving to this loony bin or that, sitting in hospital waiting rooms, three-way in-

terviews with headshrinkers, have limited the conversation. I can't just say casually, "How's your head?" All these
years my mother and I have never yet spoken directly about
her craziness; when she's high I can't get a word in edge-
wise, and when she's low she's down too deep to hear, and
so self-accusatory that one more home truth about the life
she's led herself and all of us would be too cruel, even if it
sank in in the first place. And when she's normal, more or
less, she doesn't remember, or claims she doesn't, what it's
like to be around the bend. "Did I do that? I don't recall a
thing about it." End of conversation.

But I recall one time when she was particularly high and
obnoxious I wrote her a letter in desperation and took it to
her, in an attempt to get her to face up to her erratic and
irrational behavior, but she glared at me with those opaque,
shiny eyes and tore it up, daring me to say out loud to her
face that anything was, had been, or ever would be wrong
with her. I couldn't do it. Confronted with that blank wall of
denial, what could I say? Ever since my father died—that
gay, handsome, golden man who was her whole life—she's
been running away, unable to see his death as anything but
a betrayal, a treachery, a failure, either on his part or hers.
She's never been able to put it down as just a death, one of
life's accidents. It's still right there behind her, and if she
reaches back to straighten her stocking seams or fix her
hair or zip her dress up all the way she may just by mistake
put a hand on it, that one monstrous, unacceptable, ines-
capable fact of his death. Listening to her now, filling in the
details of her discovery and operation, I realize that all
these years I've been seeing her as a paper doll, flat as a

label someone's soaked off a bottle, all front, all surface, as thin and fragile as a butterfly pinned to a board. And now there's this.

"Are you still there?" she asks.

"I'm still here."

"Aunt Helen came to see me, and you know what she said?"

"What?"

"She said, 'Well, dearie, you've got to die of something. Now you know.' Do you believe it? She was trying to be comforting. 'You've got to die of something!' I had to laugh." My mother laughs. "And you know, she's right. I always wondered what it would be, and now I know. It's a real relief."

"Wait a minute." The bells are clanging and the lights are flashing. Is she trying to tell me something? "Is that what the doctors say?"

"Oh, no. It doesn't have anything to do with them. The surgeon said he got it all and it was early and not to worry. But they always say that, and anyway, it's not the point. The point is, it's just a relief. You have no idea."

She's right. I don't. I've got to stop and think this one over, so I murmur something sympathetic about taking it easy, to which she answers, sounding mildly annoyed, what else does she have to do? I say I'll talk to her tomorrow and hang up.

Such a relief. And suddenly I'm overwhelmed with pity for her, after years and years of trying to draw a line between us, not getting too close, so I won't get dragged down or hurt. For years I haven't even thought of her as a mother so much as someone I'm detached from yet still bound to in some remote way involving loyalty and responsibility, but not sympathy and certainly not love, no, never love. I'm not really prepared for this surge of sympathy, this sudden sense of connection. I'm suspicious of it, just as I'm suspicious of her stoic, matter-of-fact, accepting tone.

I sit there clutching the phone, thinking to myself, This is finally the real thing. She's discovered a lump, gone to the doctor, had it biopsied, had the diagnosis, the mastectomy, made arrangements for radiation therapy, all by herself. It's every woman's nightmare, and all these years she had been the collapsing doll, dancing to a tune no one else could hear, falling in a heap or flying through the ceiling, manufacturing her own nightmares. Yet she's taken this in stride, on her own, and is still on her feet. Of course, as my brother Vic reminds me on the phone half an hour later, it's still too soon to tell. So the three of us keep up the phonothon, the long-distance dial-a-vigil, the wires zinging with "Well, how did her voice sound to you?" and "What's your reading of that?" and so forth, into the third week.

But at last the wires slack off; there's been no change. Fran is running her lab in Colorado, Vic's gone back to courting his English girl friend in Baltimore, and I'm still at home in Vermont with Phil and the kids.

It's odd, but I feel closer to her than I have since I can remember, perhaps closer than I ever have before. Here is the reward, I seem to be saying to her in my mind, for being straight for once, for being a good soldier. I forgive you, and I love you.

Thinking of her now, for the first time in years I want to see her instead of feeling that I have to. I picture her sitting in her chair by the window, all by herself, calmly knitting up a size 56 sweater for the fat man who lives next door. She's not running and she's not falling down, she's just knitting, with a serene, satisfied look on her face, as though she's finally got everything figured out and there's nothing to run and hide from anymore.

VII

As I pull the car into the driveway I can see her sitting in the window, so shadowy pale she's almost like a reflection. She's looking down, either reading or knitting, but as the tires crunch over the broken bits of the concrete runners she looks up and smiles expectantly. "Look, there's Grandma in the window," I say to the kids, and they both sit up and peer curiously through the car window. We haven't been here in over two years, since the summer before her operation. David barely remembers her, and Linnie not at all, but they're interested.

It's been a long trip, but I just feel tired, not particularly apprehensive. She's been so eager to see us, and I've gotten several letters in the past few weeks telling about her progress with the spring cleaning, how she's washed curtains and all the bedding. The beds have been made for two weeks, and she's laid in peanut butter, tuna fish, and chocolate chip cookies. It all sounds good. For a while in the spring I worried that she had stopped taking her lithium again, but when all three of us questioned her about it long distance, in spite of her outrage she announced that she would continue to take it, even though it made her "feel funny," just to keep peace in the family. When I told Phil the part about feeling funny, he said, "Sure, what she

means is normal. She feels normal, and to her that's funny."
Phil's away for a few weeks, and it seems like a good time to
visit; he and my mother have never gotten along.

We all get out of the car, and in the noise of multiple
doors slamming I don't hear her come out of the house, but
as I come around the back of the car to get the suitcases
she's standing there. I'm surprised at how gray she is now;
her hair, peppery-black until just a few years ago, is suddenly white, and there is a gray cast to her skin, or is it just
the last afternoon shadow, the sun gone down behind the
house? Linnie flings her arms around her and and says "Hi,
Grandma," and my mother looks down, mildly startled,
then pleased. David will not hug her; he is too shy, but I'm
touched by Linnie's instant acceptance of this strange
grandma as someone fond and huggable. For years David
has distinguished her from his other grandmother by calling her "Funny Grandma." Phil and I have never dared ask
whether he meant funny ha-ha or funny peculiar, but
we've discouraged him from calling her that to her face.
But he surprises me; seeing Linnie hug her he too with
some caution sidles up to her and puts an arm around her
back, lays his head briefly against her arm. She looks at me
proudly, eagerly. "Hi," she says.

The children run off and I move closer to her, put my arm
around her, and kiss the air next to her cheek, the way
we've always done. She steps back and says, "I didn't know
when you'd get here. How was the drive?" She sounds
slightly breathless, expectant, and as she turns to go back
inside I notice the flatness on one side of her dress. She has
gotten rather stout in the last few years, and although she
has joked to me on the telephone about not wearing a

"falsie"—"I've been flat all my life and now I can see the advantage. I'll never miss it"—the difference is obvious. But that doesn't really matter. What strikes me is that everything seems so normal at last. Here I am, a grown woman with two young children, visiting Grandma while my husband is away, just like anybody else. She looks and sounds normal, and there aren't going to be any bad surprises.

Later, after the kids have settled down to watch cartoons, we're cleaning up the kitchen and she says to me casually, "Have you heard from Phil?"

"Yes, as a matter of fact. He called from London Sunday night. Everything's fine."

"I used to do what you're doing after your father died, you know."

I look up startled. "What's that?"

"Take trips with you kids. It was so lonely, especially around holidays, and no one in the family ever invited us anywhere, and I got so I couldn't stand it, so I'd just throw you kids in the car and take off."

I sit there flabbergasted. The last thing I want after all these years is to find out how much I'm like my mother. I remember the strange feeling I had taking the kids through Old Sturbridge Village a few days ago. I had to keep reminding myself that I was the grown-up, that I had to take the responsibility for keeping everybody together and safe and happy, and I felt a strange reluctance. I had to force myself to assume the grown-up role, and I felt that I was walking around as much in costume as all the guides in their old-fashioned clothes. One of the places my mother took us when my sister and brother and I were children was

Sturbridge, and now I try to remember if what I felt there two days ago could be related to being there before, having to assume the grown-up role in spite of myself, when I wasn't grown up. When I go there with my real children, the past haunts me, lies in wait for me in a way I don't even suspect.

"I don't like myself this way, you know," my mother says abruptly.

"Like what?"

Without a word she pulls up her sweater and shows me the hollow where her breast used to be, with the scar running across horizontally. The scar is barely noticeable—it's been almost two years since the operation—but the skin is stretched over bone, and I'm surprised to see how much flesh my mother has everywhere else in contrast to this hollow place, because I have always thought of her as a thin, angular person. I don't know what to say. She has said so many times that it didn't matter, that she hardly missed it. "Just like this," she answers, pulling down her sweater. "And old. I seem to have gotten old and gray all of a sudden. I don't like to look at myself in the mirror." I remember that not long after the operation she wrote me to send her giant-sized bath towels for her birthday, and I realize now they were to cover herself up, not from everybody else's eyes but from her own. I want to tell her I'm sorry, but I can't; it's not enough. I go around the table and put my arms around her to hug her, but she stands rigid, away from me. I hug her anyway, then sit down. Physical expression of sympathy is easier, even though we're unused to it; I can't say anything that will help. The next thing I do is turn practical, as always the problem solver, the troubleshooter, the fastest gun. So I aim for the source, or what I assume is the source.

"Why don't you get a breast form?"

She turns away from me, and her eyelids drop, but just before they do I catch a glimpse of the old evasive look. "What's the point? Why put up a false front? It really doesn't matter at my age. I just want to die and get it over with."

The words are so familiar, the refrain of so many of my years, that in spite of my determinedly practical "here's a problem and we'll solve it, where there's life there's hope" attitude, I find myself getting angry. I really thought she'd gotten past that. So I ignore the practical approach and address her last remark. "Don't tell me you still feel that way, even after all these years?"

She turns back but doesn't look at me. "Of course, I have ever since your father died."

"Doesn't it mean something to you to have survived? Isn't there some satisfaction in that, in being a survivor?"

She looks me straight in the eye for an instant, and before she hoods them, her eyes fix me with an eagle look I've never seen before, proud, watchful, and without hope. Then the look is gone, and I'm not even sure I've seen it.

"No," she says matter-of-factly. "Everyone I ever loved except you kids has died, so why shouldn't I?"

Her words leave me speechless. I just sit there stupidly, nodding my head as though I understand, sympathize, when in fact it's all I can do to hold my eyelids apart, because if I blink the tears that have rushed up behind them will fall out, and my mother will see me cry. I take a breath, get up from the table, and turn away, pretending to fold the newspaper. As I stand there, it strikes me that I can't remember when she has said to me in so many words, "I love you." This is the closest she has ever come. I want to turn and say, But if you love me, us, and we're not dead, aren't we enough, haven't we ever been enough, can't you go on from here and try to be happy with what you have left, with just being alive? Not even for us, not even for me? I stand there rattling the newspaper, my lips clamped together, and the moment passes. I have done nothing to break through the long silence, the barrier we've put up between us down the years of crying in the night in separate rooms.

"Well, I guess I'll go to bed," I say casually. "Tomorrow is another day."

She looks at me and smiles. "You must be tired. So much excitement and such a long way. And tomorrow is another day."

"Good night, Mom."

"Good night, Sara. I'm glad you're here."

I'd planned to stay four or five days, but by the middle of the next day it's clear that things aren't going to work out. It's raining, and the kids have opened all their presents, explored the attic and basement, and now are asking for things to do. I had thought that the four of us might go someplace, visit the zoo or drive around the lake, but when I ask my mother if she wants to go, if she has any suggestions, she says no. "Don't you want to do anything with the children?" I ask, annoyed because she's urged us to come, looked forward to our visit, and now just sits in her chair as though we weren't here.

"I don't do things with children, I just like to watch them," she answers imperturbably, and goes on knitting. I begin to feel more than annoyed. As a matter of fact, I'm getting quite angry, so I turn and go upstairs, away from her, from the children bickering on the floor. How alien everything seems, how unreal—the way my mother lives. I walk through the upstairs alone and touch a crack in the plaster, and it comes away in my hand, a cobweb. Cobwebs heavy with dust festoon the corners of the rooms, the tops of the curtains, drape the lampshades. Last night I turned on the bedside lamp and smelled the dusty odor of dead flies smoldering in the heat of the light bulb. The surfaces are clean, the tops of tables and dressers, the rugs and parts of floors that show, but under the dresser scarves my grandmother embroidered the dust has sifted through the eyelets and made a stenciled pattern on the wood, and the underneaths and corner places of the house are barricaded with dust. Nothing has changed.

As the day goes on I grow more and more irritable with the children. My mother sits and wants me to sit, wants to talk about old times; she doesn't see people very often, and it's such a treat to have someone to talk to, she says. The children don't want to listen to our talk, they want me to play with them. They wander in and out of the room, little phantoms interrupting, and their voices wind higher and more imploring. "What can I do now? Will you play with me? I'm bored." I reprove, then scold them, telling them to take care of themselves for once, not to interrupt, and after a while I begin to hear my mother's voice in mine, the same intonations of irritability, impatience, beyond what is justified by the children's behavior. I wonder if I really sound like her all the time and just don't notice when I'm not with her, or if I'm beginning to imitate her.

The weather clears, and finally I take the kids to the lake for the afternoon, and immediately the feeling of being pulled down, suffocated, mummified in cobwebs lifts, and I resume my own relation to reality, talking to our old friend who owns the cottage where we swim. But then it's time to go back for dinner. We troop into the house and my mother is still sitting; there is no dinner. She gets up stiffly, reluctantly, making odd guttural noises like a squawking bird, and stands in the middle of the room, lifting and stretching her legs. I'm standing in the kitchen when I hear Linnie let out a howl, then I hear her small feet hurrying up the stairs, accompanied by sobs. I brush past my mother, go upstairs after Linnie, who's in bed with the covers pulled over her head. The covers vibrate with silent weeping. I sit on the bed, put my hand on her little round rump under the blanket.

"What's the matter, honey?"

"I don't want to tell you."

"Oh, Linnie, you can tell me."

She claws the covers off her tear-blotched face and looks at me, lips quivering.

"Grandma slapped me in the face."

I go still suddenly, but my stomach lurches. "Why?" I say as calmly as I can.

"For no reason." She turns her face into the pillow and covers her eyes with her hands and sobs.

And I remember all the times, the helpless, bewildering times "for no reason" when I could not understand what my mother was doing or why, why she was so angry, what she wanted from us, how to behave so that she would be like other mothers, when my anxious questions brought

83

only the furious answer "Because I say so" or no answer at all. I'm caught now between my mother and my children, and I'm alone, all alone, the one who has to make things right. I feel like I'm seventeen all over again, standing alone between my mother and my younger sister and brother, trying to save them, save myself, and all at once I'm a climber, veering, springing away up a cliff of loose stones, scrambling and sliding, trying to get away, crying "Not again, not anymore." But I stop clawing upward, let myself slide back slowly down the rock. This time I really am the grown-up, not a child desperately trying to mimic one out of confusion and despair. I'm not helpless, and I won't run. I bend over and kiss Linnie's shiny cheek, hold her body under the covers.

"Don't worry, I'll take care of you. It will be all right." Linnie nods and smiles, shuts her eyes, and pops her thumb into her mouth with a sigh.

I go downstairs. David is sitting at the kitchen table reading the funny papers, unaware that anything is wrong. My mother is standing at the sink, peeling potatoes.

"Did you hit Linnie?" I ask, trying to keep my voice level.

Deliberately, without looking at me, she says, "She came up and started punching me in the stomach. I tapped her lightly across the face. It was a reflex, automatic. Self-defense." Her tone implies exasperation, as if she really ought not to have to explain this, it's so simple.

My ears roar and I shut my eyes. I speak very softly. "She's upstairs crying. She's very upset. I don't think she understands the concept of self-defense. Please don't do it again. I don't care whether it's a reflex or not." My mother nods, sticks out her lower lip, and goes on peeling potatoes.

I sit down at the table with David, who looks at me curiously. My mother puts the potatoes in a pot on the stove, starts past me. "I'll be right back," she says. "I just have to go to the bathroom."

I hear her go upstairs. Then David asks me to read him some of the funnies. It's a while before I realize that my mother has not come right back. I hear the bed creaking upstairs in the room Linnie and I share. I get up from the table and go quickly, silently up the stairs, and when I reach the doorway of our room my mother is sitting on the bed, holding Linnie's arms, struggling with her, shaking and pushing her, pinning her to the bed. Linnie's eyes are fixed on her face, and they are wild and panicky with speechless, uncomprehending terror. My mother is saying quietly, "I just want to wrestle with you, get rid of some of that excess energy, show you a little self-defense. Come on, push me away, try to push me away." Her voice sounds gentle, but I can't see her face, and Linnie can, and she's afraid. Then Linnie catches sight of me and she takes a huge sobbing desperate breath; her eyes flood with relief. In one step I reach the bed, push my mother out of the way, and snatch Linnie up in my arms, safe. She winds her arms and legs around me and buries her head in my shoulder with a trembling sigh, and I walk out of the room with her.

"Grandma was scaring me. I'm so glad you came," she whispers brokenly. I walk down the stairs, holding Linnie, and call to David in the kitchen. "Come on, David, we're going out." My mother reaches the bottom of the stairs just as I am about to go out the door with the children. Over Linnie's head I look at her. She stares back, her lower lip jutting out defensively. "I was just trying to cheer her up," she says. She weaves as though she has been drinking, and her eyes are cloudy, opaque, as though the cobwebs have grown in them too. And I realize in a split second of bursting rage that I haven't forgiven her a thing. Whatever I thought or dreamed I had forgiven her for myself I will never forgive for my children. "Well, you didn't," I tell her. "We're going out."

"Are you coming back?" she asks. Her speech is slurred. It occurs to me that she has probably not been taking her pills. I turn away. She has let me down again, let my children down. "Of course I'll be back," I say crossly. "Take your pill." She blinks, then gives me that haughty race-horse look. I put Linnie down, go to the sink, dump out one of her lithium pills, fill a glass of water, and walk back to my mother, holding the pill in one hand and the glass in the other. My mother takes the pill and drinks the water, still glaring at me. "Well," she says, "I'm going to bed. I'm simply exhausted. Have a nice time." She turns and marches back up the stairs, while the children and I go out the door.

Later, after we've come home and the children are asleep, I lie in bed trying to get hold of myself. My body feels enormous, taut and heavy with rage; my heart pounds, my chest hurts, and my forehead is tight. I feel like the stone giant I've told the children about, the carved statue, once supposed to be a petrified man, buried in a field not far from here many years ago as a hoax. The giant lies on his side, his legs drawn up, his arms over his stomach as if in pain, but he's frozen into stone, and the weight bears him down into the earth, paralyzed, stiff, and cold. My hands and feet are numb, creeping into stone. I feel like crying out, but there's no one to call to, not even anyone to whisper to about how awful it is. Phil's not here to comfort me, there's me, just me, and then the hot tears start rolling down my cheeks and I cry silently, not wanting to wake Linnie. It's the same old pattern, nothing ever changes, and I was a fool to risk them too. But how I've longed for it to be all right, if not for me, for them. I didn't realize it was too late.

But then a sound, a cough, some restless shifting from the next room catches my attention. On the other side of the wall my mother is awake. But what good does it do, I think to myself, even if she is awake? She's inaccessible, out of reach. I've given her up. I can't talk to her. I've never talked to her about anything that mattered, about her illness, about how I felt; it's always been just like this, the wall between us and the two of us lying alone, each in our own separate distress. I toss and turn, listening to my stomach churn, trying to relax, but I'm really listening to her. And then, listening, trying to puzzle out the sounds and what they mean, I feel a sudden impulse to break the pattern. I've got to know for sure what's going on in there.

I get out of bed, walk across the room and into the hall, knock lightly and push open her door. She's lying on her side in bed, watching television. "Yeah, hi," she says eagerly. Her voice sounds perfectly normal. I feel my stomach loosen. I step forward cautiously.

"What's the matter? Can't you sleep?"

She flips a hand dismissively, then tucks it behind her head, the elbow pointed to the ceiling. I've often seen her lie like this, relaxed, expectant.

"I go to sleep, then I wake up and I can't get back to sleep, so I just lie awake. Can't you sleep?"

"No, not right now." I sit down in a chair at the foot of her bed. "Does it bother you?"

"Oh, no. I don't mind a bit. I think about my life. It doesn't bother me a bit. I've got lots to think about." She reaches over and turns off the sound of the television.

"What do you think about?"

She smiles. "Oh, lots of things. About when I was a child, and my college days." She puts the other arm behind her head, lies back, and chuckles. "Did I ever tell you about the time . . ." And she begins to tell me a story about the time she was president of the Woman's Athletic Association at Syracuse, and went to the chancellor to get the budget raised, and got it cut back instead. It's the first of several stories of her life before she was married, stories I've never heard, and she tells them humorously, without stopping, while the light from the television flickers over her face. I listen and watch her face for a long time. She's all right, she's really all right, in spite of all the bad signs and my own fierce condemning anger. And I'm glad I came in to see for myself, glad I'm not a helpless and bewildered child anymore, afraid of what I'll find. After a while I say good night and go back to my room. We haven't talked about anything important, but it strikes me that we've just talked about ordinary things the way I've always imagined other mothers and daughters might do, as though all the years of struggling and wrestling back and forth between us had never existed. I lie in bed and think about my mother and me. I haven't forgiven her, but I begin to see that perhaps it's not a matter of forgiveness after all. It's not anyone's fault, really, this separation, this lack: not hers, not mine. It

seems so simple, and the words revolve together in my
head as I fall asleep.

Finally, it's time to leave, the bags are packed and in the
car, my mother's arthritis is kicking up and she's coming
down with a cold, but she gets up briefly to say goodbye to
us, standing in her bathrobe with her hair flat and mussed.
The children both come toward her to kiss her goodbye but
she fends them off, saying, "Don't kiss me; you'll catch my
cold." Neither of them seems particularly affected by what
has gone on; Linnie fastidiously screws up her face as
though shutting her eyes and mouth tight could keep out
germs, but throws her arms around my mother's body and
hugs her close. David does the same, ducking his head. But
something holds me back. Maybe it's her own statement;
I'm so tired of reading between the lines that now I'm prepared to take her at her word. If she doesn't want me to kiss
her goodbye, I won't. In spite of our talk last night I still feel
alienated, separated from her. We haven't touched; our
pasts don't touch; we've never admitted what's gone on between us all these years. The truth is, I've worn out the thin
fabric of my unquestioning childhood love, and what is
left? There are too many cobwebs here, too many echoes,
cries of past and present misery, confusion and despair, and
no one sees or hears them but me. My mother isn't crazy
now; she's perfectly all right, but I don't like it here, and
I'm not staying. The leap of sympathy I felt exists only in
my imagination; in real life, face to face, it doesn't come. I
can't talk to her now, I never could, and I never will. It isn't
right between us, and there's nothing I can do to make it
so. That's not forgiveness, but recognition will just have to

do. I'm on my way out the door when my mother calls out, "Sara, wait!" and groans and creaks her way upstairs. She comes back, holds out her hands to me. Rolling in the middle of the palm is a single gold bead. She smiles apologetically. "I found it in my shoe. It must have gotten stuck in there. I've been saving it for you. Maybe now the beads will fit." I take the bead and squeeze her hand. "Goodbye, Mom. I'll be seeing you."

As I pull the car out of the driveway I look back. My mother stands in the driveway facing me as I'm about to drive away. I haven't kissed her goodbye, or even hugged her. She looks old, frail, bedraggled, and sad. It occurs to me that she's not serene, she's beaten. Now that the space between us is widening again, I feel once more a stab of pity. I stop the car and wave. She continues to stare blankly into space. What's wrong? Then I realize she can't see far enough to tell I'm waving at her. I honk the horn, flail my hand out the window. She jumps slightly, then her face lights up and she smiles, the nearsighted public smile for the audience up front she's not quite sure is there. It's a nice smile, and she waves an odd, jaunty, flipflop wave in our direction, But not at me, not at the real me, no, never, not at me.

IN ANOTHER COUNTRY

Lying half asleep on the couch in the waiting room, staring into the closet someone has left open in which mine is now the only coat, I listen to the sound of rough irregular breathing, trying to measure my own against it. This is impossible; however compelling, the rhythm is inappropriate for sustaining life, the pauses too long, the breaths too short. A radiator suffers in the background, snuffling and shuddering. Overhead, a circulating fan hums its white noise. *Suck, sigh, swish, thump.* It's not somebody trying to breathe, of course, it's the pneumatic doors of the intensive care unit opening and closing. The breathing is irregular because it's late at night now—not so many comings and goings. The doctor has been coming in every half hour, but now he's not. At first he stayed in his greens, just in case,

91

but the last time he showed up in a business suit, mildly redolent of gin. I interpret this as a good sign, but I could be wrong. Later on, when I am better at this, I will be able to sort out all the signs, good and bad. Names and places, for instance. The names of some of these places do not mince words: Trauma Center, Critical Care Unit, Post-Recovery Room, Step-Down Floor. Some of them, A-2, E-3, are names in code. But some of them are named for people: the Harvey Randall Unit, the Mary Moore Memorial Pavilion, as well as their concomitant waiting rooms, the Hill solarium, the Fischbein foyer, the Gardner family area—personal memorials combined with friendly euphemisms, allaying anxiety, forestalling panic. Uh, where am I? In Mary Moore. Oh, really? Thank you very much. Much better than waking up to find yourself in Intensive Care, or in the waiting room next door.

Though the sign outside this particular pneumatic door says discreetly SPECIAL CARE, the nurses and doctors call it ICU, and here the patients get exactly that—the full-time persistent attentions and constant ministrations of as many of the best nurses available at this time in this place as necessary, doctors swinging in and out at any and all hours, barking orders for this and that test and procedure, *stat*. Round-the-clock visiting hours, five minutes in the hour, only the immediate family, no children under eighteen please, just like an X-rated movie. There are no chairs in ICU because no one ever sits down. The nurses don't have time, the patients are too sick, and visitors are not invited. This is a stopover place; no one is supposed to stay. This is where life pauses, unable for the moment to sustain itself unaided. Life pauses here, chuffs and sighs and groans and bleeps, and then goes on to somewhere else.

II

It's ten o'clock in the morning, and I'm sitting in the hospital room they wheeled him away from a little while ago to be operated on. The nurse has assured me that if everything goes well, they'll bring him back here directly from Recovery, so this is where I've been waiting.

At last, after what seems like many hours but in fact is only three, the surgeon stalks in, dressed in a fresh clean surgical gown that rattles as he moves, some of the creases not even fully opened yet. With his long skinny legs and bulky torso, baggy-sleeved arms on his hips, he resembles a great gawky bird about to flap his wings and fly away. He looks distracted, uneasy, craning his Adam's apple out of the gown's neck as though it were choking him, Big Bird wrapped in green Kleenex, peering and blinking everywhere except at me, which I do not interpret as a good sign.

It is not. He reports that the patient won't be coming back here after all, that he lost more blood than they'd like —which they've replaced, of course—but they're mildly concerned about him and so are going to take him to Intensive Care. That's in a while; right now he's still in Recovery, getting more blood. So he's very sorry, but I can't see him yet.

I watch from the lounge chair in the corner, disappointed. I thought it would be over by now, the waiting, and I could see him. But at least he got through the operation.

Reassured that this part is over, and so fast too—isn't that a good sign?—I look up expectantly at the surgeon, waiting to hear the good news.

But he shakes his head, cranes his neck, and toes the floor. As I stare up at him, he shakes his head again, glares up at the ceiling, and shuffles his feet. "It was a bash," he says. "A really bloody bash."

My eyes rove upward past his face to the rim of his green surgeon's cap. Across it, a tiny crimson comet frozen in space, is a single, still-bright splash of blood.

I don't hear the rest of what the surgeon says; I don't even notice when he leaves. I'm convinced the patient's dying, even dead already, and they can't bring themselves to tell me yet. Don't die, I whisper, sending the signal down the corridors past all the doors of all the other rooms and into the one they call Recovery; hang on, I'm here. Come back, don't die, it's too soon, we need more time. Goddammit, it's not fair.

The nurse's aide comes in while I'm sitting there, starts to pack up his belongings in a plastic garbage bag: pajamas, Dopp kit, street clothing, aftershave, glasses, the book he was reading last night, bookmark and all. "He won't be coming back here," she says noncommittally as she shakes the bag down, twists the top, closes it with a plastic tab, and slings it in a corner next to the door. She grabs a dust mop and starts to clean the floor, pushing the bed around with one hip and swabbing underneath. Looking at the lumpy contours of the trash bag I can't help myself, the tears sting upward, and I start to cry, loud wet disreputable sobs. The aide continues mopping, uninterested, pushing the small pile of debris closer and closer to my feet, as though she would like to push me out as well.

Finally she says, not unkindly, "Excuse me, but we need the room. I'm afraid you'll have to go somewhere else. There's a nice waiting room right down the hall."

So I stand up, wipe my tears, hoist up the bag, and move on, to the nice waiting room down the hall.

III

After some argument, they let me visit him as soon as they've taken him into ICU, even though he's still unconscious. I see him as soon as I walk in. He is in the center unit, right in front of the nurse's station, lying not on a bed but on some sort of stretcher too short for him, too narrow, so that even now he looks bigger and more imposing than he is, as though the stretcher can barely hold his weight. Except for his size and the darkness of his hair, I would never be able to pick him out, he is so pale, his otherwise naked body so obscured by all the tubes and wires going into his arms, his neck, his feet, sticking out from his side, from the bruised limp tube of flesh between his legs. There is a vacuum-cleaner hose down his throat, so that his head is thrust back, his eyes open to a shiny saurian serpentine slit, octopus suckers on his chest attached to wires that lead to a machine that bleeps a rapid noise, scrabbles across a screen a line as furred as tinsel. Digital numbers flash—two-twenty. Is that possible? A pulse rate of two-twenty? There must be some mistake; nobody, not even he, the jogger, the athlete, can keep that up for long. Slow down, I mutter to the machine, to the frenzied fist inside his chest, willing the tinsel line to unfur itself a little, the green bleep to slow down. Standing in the center of the middle section, my eyes are riveted on the screen, watching for some change. Slow down, but for God's sake don't stop. Still it goes on, the dancing point, impossibly fast, almost a solid bleep, and the respirator shunts and sighs like a tuneless electric hurdy-gurdy, and the nurse is occupied in trying to spread a hospital gown over all the wires and tubes while she pumps up the blood pressure cuff with her free hand.

And suddenly I am overwhelmed by the sense that I have blundered into a wrong room somewhere, that I don't belong here and must leave as gracefully as possible, and I stand grinning like an idiot in the center of the wrong place, looking everywhere but at the figure on the stretcher, hoping no one will notice me before I have a chance to exit inconspicuously. But I can't move. His nurse is frowning now, concentrating, the stethoscope pressed to the crook of his elbow. She moves it quickly to his neck, listens, stops frowning, turns to write something down, removes the stethoscope from her ears but leaves the cuff around his arm, glances quickly at all the machines and dials, prods a bag hung overhead, one of several, some with dark liquid, some with clear, then catches sight of me.

"Hi," she says matter-of-factly. "You can stay if you want, but he's still out cold. There's really nothing you can do, we're pretty busy with him now, but if you want to wait outside, I'll have someone come and get you if there's any change." She smiles briefly, while her eyes dart watchfully from dial to dial and bag to bag.

I back away, eyes fixed on the heart monitor, willing the green dot to slow down and not exhaust itself, watching the terrorized line leap up and down in frenzy, while behind me as I back up another bleep begins to slow down, sputters, hops once or twice, then sinks to the center and hums a steady tune. I turn to see a flat line run across a nearby monitor. Just like in the movies, I think, on the verge of giggling, and then a sudden horror overwhelms me: my God, people *die* in here. A nurse comes over to the bed, reaches up, and yanks a white curtain around, enveloping herself inside. I turn around again, am reassured by the frenzied but, yes, still steady bleeping of his heart, the rising and falling of his chest.

"I just wanted to see him," I blurt out like an idiot. "I thought he might be dead."

His nurse looks up, smiles briefly in her impassive way, and says, "Don't worry. He's fighting very hard."

And his flesh is wound around his bones as frail as smoke, and there is nothing I can do but wait.

I turn and walk through the pneumatic doors, back into the waiting room, humming a tune that has just now popped into my head, drowning out the other noises. As I sit in the next room, waiting to be sent for, I hum it over and over, trying to place it. But it's only a few bars of the refrain, and hard as I try to remember I get no further than these repeated words: "Everyone's gone to the moo—oon, everyone's gone to the moon."

IV

In the waiting room, I imagine this:

He first feels the pain as a hot twinge in his wrist, then down his arm from the shoulder like a red-hot zipper being closed; the tightening in his chest comes last. Suddenly he

97

is aware of his heart as a fist, clenching and unclenching in rhythm, squeezing harder and harder, then perversely refusing to let go, so that all the blood rushing to be squeezed has nowhere else to go and backs up, starts to pool and distend the veins, puts pressure on his lungs, pressure on his heart and down his arm, pressure on his stomach so he feels sick. Let go, he says, but it will not let go. Congestion, dizziness, pain, sweat, anxiety. Still, it's nothing. A little heartburn. Nothing to worry about. Save my room, he tells the hotel clerk from the stretcher as they take him out to the ambulance. Save my room. I'll be back tomorrow.

Of course that is not what really happened, but that is how I think it must have seemed to him: nothing unusual, just a little worse. After all, it was not as though he had never felt anything like this before. Once or twice on the golf course, at the top of his swing, a tightness resisting, at the top of a ladder reaching up to paint the eaves, a time or two on the stairs walking up to his office. Always it had gone away, leaving him only momentarily gray-faced and short of breath. Still, he had just been to the doctor not two weeks before. I went with him; we both had appointments for routine checkups, his for a touch of indigestion and heartburn, mine a physical for camp.

The doctor examines me first, while my father stands there watching, eternally vigilant. But when it's his turn they make me leave.

"Why can't I stay, Daddy?" I demand. "I want to watch. You watched me."

"See you later," he says.

"If you'll excuse us," the doctor says.

"It's not fair," I say.

"Go on," my father says sternly, inclining his head toward the door. The doctor opens the door and ushers me out. I go out into the waiting room in a huff and sit down next to the fish tank, feeling cross, wondering why they won't let me stay and watch, what my father doesn't want me to see. Meanwhile, the two of them are chuckling behind the door, which makes me even crosser. Determined to ignore them with their secrets, I fold my arms across my chest and glare at the tropical fish swimming around in their murky bowl. Round and round they go, the brightly colored fish in their little glass bowl, strings of air bubbles going straight up. I stare fixedly at them as they revolve around the little stone castle in the middle. They remind me of the merry-go-round at Walbridge Park, the big amusement park not far from our house, where my parents often take us in the summer. In fact, we were there just the other day; every year on Memorial Day, the day the rides open, and if you're lucky you can catch a gold ring on the merry-go-round good for free rides all summer.

I'm on the merry-go-round, a big old-fashioned one partly enclosed in a shed, with a huge brightly painted steam calliope in the center, hooting and hissing, a giant hurdy-gurdy, and I'm riding the big black horse on the outside, while my father and mother stand to one side watching me. My sister and brother have had enough of the merry-go-round; they are too little to ride alone, and sitting with my mother in the sleigh is boring, so they stand there next to my parents eating cotton candy and getting sticky. But I can ride alone, and because I have not gotten off between rides, I have finally managed to jostle and push my way up onto my favorite horse, the one I secretly call Black

Beauty. He has a real bridle and reins, and I hold onto the reins, not the pole the way the younger children do, plunging and leaping, round and round while the calliope thumps and groans in the middle and the rods overhead pump and churn the animals up and down.

The bell rings and the merry-go-round slows down, stops. A cheer goes up as everyone looks over toward a young man walking along the sidelines carrying a wire basket full of shiny metal rings. He steps up onto a platform next to a hollow bar that sticks out at one side of the shed toward the back, and empties the basket into a hopper at the top of the slanted bar. I can hear the rings rolling down the chute until the bar is full, and one ring is clearly visible, sticking out of the little bit-out semicircle at the lower end. He sets the spring that will pop the rings out one after another as they're caught, and stands to one side, watching. The crowd murmurs, the riders look at each other, smiling slyly, wondering which one of us will get the gold ring. As the merry-go-round starts to revolve, spin counterclockwise toward the bar, all the riders on the outside lean as far out as they can, right arms extended, index fingers pointing, trying to snare the ring. I can hear the screams and shouts, the exclamations of disappointment, for it is too dark inside the shed to see whether the ring is brass or gold until it is on your finger, and once you have a ring you aren't allowed to try again. The spring clicks rapidly as the rings move down the slot and are snatched away. I lean out as far as I can, holding onto the pole now, hearing the calliope bump and snort, feeling the horse leap and plunge, my eyes fixed on the ring as I come around out of the bright sunlight into the shade. I pass my father, grinning, his arms folded.

"Reach, Sara, reach," I hear him call, and I lean out far, stretch my arm out, finger extended. But even though I am twelve years old now, my arm is still too short. I have missed the ring by at least six inches, and I am already hanging practically sideways in my saddle, with one leg barely hooked over. I feel the tears start, and I see my father nodding and smiling as I whirl by again, fair hair gleaming in the sunlight that casts my mother's face into the familiar lines and angles, and as I go by I shout in a fury of disappointment, "I can't reach! I'm not big enough! I can't!"

"Come on, Sara!" my father calls out. "Try again. There's no such word as can't!"

"Daddy!" I scream, looking back desperately over my shoulder as I pass around the back. But as I come around again, I see my father start to run alongisde the merry-go-round, step up and swing himself onto a riderless horse bobbing up and down several rows ahead of me. He looks back over his shoulder and smiles, and as I stare at him, he leans out and out, his long arm stretched wide, finger crooked, and I am so happy because I know the gold ring is next—

—And my father swings out closer, leaping and plunging as I plunge and leap, and the ring is there, there, my father snatches back his hand, clutching it hidden to his chest, looking back over his shoulder at me with an odd expression. Did you get it? I shout as we wheel and plunge and whirl, but suddenly I'm dizzy and maybe even a little sick, and I have to shut my eyes for a second. When I open them I see my father still in front, but inexplicably he seems to be pulling away from me on his leaping plunging horse, farther and farther ahead, still looking back at me with his hand clutched to his chest, the same odd expression on his face. Wait for me! I shout. Did you get it? I call to him excitedly. Did you get the ring? What is it? But he rounds the far side of the merry-go-round behind the big steam calliope and disappears, and I don't know whether he has the ring or not, and the music thumps louder and louder, groans and chuffs and bleeps, and the horses go faster and faster, round and round—*and he goes out the door and down the steps: Come back—*

"Sara." I jerk up, my father's hand on my shoulder. I'm sitting in the chair in the doctor's waiting room, next to the goldfish bowl. "Time to go," my father says to me, and I stand up. I look at him; he looks the same. "What is it?" I ask, bewildered by his presence. My father smiles, and pats my arm. "Nothing much. Just a little touch of indigestion. You're fine too. Let's go."

And I still wonder why they made me leave. Did he know what it really was? Was it modesty on his part, or was he really hiding something from me? Would I have noticed what the doctor didn't, that it wasn't heartburn at all, but a heart about to burn itself out? If I had been there, would I have known, and done something? Would I, could I, would I?

So they have taken him away to the intensive care unit of the hospital in a city far from home, hooked him up to the respirator and the oxygen tent and the heart monitor, with tubes and wires and electrodes, but just the same, he knows he will be back and the motel manager should save his room, because he has unfinished business here. No need to call my wife, thank you, I'll be back.

Now he lies in the hospital oxygen tent, with the tubes,

the wires, the lines, the machines, the nurses hovering. He is unconscious now, and no one waits beside him. I am, as always, still too far away, for this is long ago and in another country, and besides, the patient's dead.

V

"Why is he shaking like that?" I ask the doctor, because his whole body, swathed in its net of wires and tubes and drains, is shaking violently in spasms, rattling the wires and tubes, making the little green line spike up and down in peaks and valleys that freeze in my mind like icicles on a roof. His eyelids are fluttering, his teeth rattle like dice in a shaker, the respirator tube writhes like a snake across his chest, and I can see his throat working up and down against it. I stand next to the bed mesmerized with horror; if he wasn't dying before, I think to myself, he certainly is now.

"He's shivering," the surgeon answers; then, noticing my incredulous, possibly even scornful look, adds, "because he's cold."

"He's *cold?*" I suppress a wild little hoot of laughter; the answer is so absurdly simple. "But it's so hot in here."

The doctor stands, hands in his pockets, contemplating his patient. "His body temperature's low, from his insides being exposed to the air all that time. You lose a lot of body heat that way. Even though we keep the temperature as high as we can, we can't keep it at ninety-eight point six. Everybody'd pass out. He'll warm up once his system gets over the shock." His face is impassive as he contemplates his patient, stretched as pale and flaccid as some long-dead sea creature washed up on the sand. His eyes are used to this. He stands for a moment longer, then catches the nurse's eye, nods to her. She comes over to him, inclines her head attentively as he says something in a voice too low for me to hear. He turns back to me. "If you'll excuse us, would you mind waiting outside for a few minutes?"

Oh, no, you don't, I want to say. Oh, no, I've heard that one before, and I'm not leaving. Not this time.

"We're going to pull that respirator tube. He's starting to fight it, which means he's ready to start breathing on his own," the doctor says, then pauses, regarding me. "It's not that nice to watch," he says after a moment. Then he shrugs the by-now considerably more rumpled shoulders of his greens. "But you're welcome to stay if you want." He turns toward the bed, where the nurse is spreading towels across the patient's chest. I turn and walk back down the hall to the waiting room, back to wondering silently what act or what omission has brought us to this place.

VI

Here is another waiting room—though they call it a family conference room here—this one in Seneca State Hospital, not too far down the hall from the locked ward where my mother spent the first several months of her stay after her breakdown in 1958. She is not in the locked ward any more, having made a great deal of progress in the eleven months she's been here, and in fact I've come to pick her up and take her home. The psychiatrists think that forty shock treatments may have done the trick; although she's still on Thorazine at the moment, she may even be able to stop that after a while. We'll see how it goes, the social worker tells me as he hands over the small box of her personal belongings, some emery boards, a toothbrush and half-used tube of toothpaste, her glasses, which she was not allowed to wear without supervision and thus were kept here, out of harm's way, some extra underwear and dresses, slippers, and a paperback copy of *Bartlett's Quotations*.

She seems a little dazed as she comes down the hall, as if she doesn't quite see me or know who I am; then I remember. "Do you want your glasses?" I ask her, but she just shakes her head and smiles at me, and I remember a story she told me about how horrified she was when she first got glasses many years ago to find that the world was not a pleasant fuzzy blurred place after all, and how long it took her to get used to its sharpness. So she will get used to it again in time.

On the way home we talk a little, but she is very quiet, subdued even, and more than a little vague about what's gone on the last few years. So she does not remember systematically demolishing the interiors of the three houses we have lived in during the six years since my father died, the three houses my grandfather built one after the other, going up the hill like steps, only one of which, unfortunately, still belongs to us; breaking in and entering the others, emptying cupboards and closets, overturning furniture, scattering trash all over, hammering holes in plaster, and running away across the fields, while I watched her slight figure becoming more and more attentuated in the fading light of dusk, until the police, directed by me, caught her almost a mile away. She remembers nothing of this, and perhaps it's just as well. They say that's what shock treatments do to you: along with the memories they wipe away the faulty electrical circuits that the brain sets up for itself and let new healthier ones establish themselves instead. One of my mother's psychiatrists at Seneca explained it to me using the analogy of a child's electric train circling round and round the same old piece of track, incessantly clicking over the same old clicks, on and on until someone turns off the juice and reroutes the layout. Driving back home, I picture a small electric train zipping around inside my mother's head, over its new layout, and hope that this time she will stay on the rails, so I won't have to pull the plug and stand there watching as she runs across the fields, away from the three ruined houses, from her children who stand watching, from my father's death, runs away inside her head as well as with her body, down the long dark corridor of her own making, as fast and as far away as she can get. But although this is her worst breakdown, it will not be the last.

And as I sit here in this other waiting room twenty years later, remembering, thinking of my own husband who may be dead or dying, and my own small children waiting at home, for a moment I don't know who is who, or where I am, and I'm afraid, because it could just as well be me running, running across those fields, somewhere, anywhere, as long as it's away. And hypnotized, exhausted by that running figure, I shut my eyes, lean my head back against the couch, and try to sleep.

I do sleep; not only that, I dream. In my dream I hear the sound of rough irregular breathing—*suck, sigh, swish*—and make myself breathe along with it, coaching him, filling my lungs and exhaling in the same hesitant rhythm, but just ahead, willing it into measured cadence, knowing that if I keep on breathing, he will keep on breathing, that together we can get from this dangerous place to where he can be trusted to breathe once more on his own. Just a little longer, hanging on. But the breathing gets more and more irregular despite my efforts, the pauses lengthen, until I can hardly hold back my own breath; I am holding my breath as though I were under water, and I begin to panic, to thrash around; I have to breathe, but the pause lengthens and there is no release. I listen attentively for the sound. Breathe, dammit. Breathe! I stare at the still chest of the prone figure, willing it to move up and down, take a breath. I reach forward, stop with my hand held out; I can't bring myself to touch. *Don't die,* I whisper, *come back,* but the words use up all my air and I drag in a huge breath in spite of myself, against my will. I exhale it quickly, listening for an echo. It does not come. All is quiet, and I know that I have failed again. I watch as the water curls up and over into a giant vacuum-cleaner hose, a mirror tunnel, rim after rim, and crashes down around the tiny figure at the far end, obliterating it. I claw my way to the surface, throw off the leaden tank that has been holding me down, break the surface, and take a great gulp of air. . . .

And wake to find myself alone in the waiting room, cramped and squeezed into a corner of the couch. I look around; the clock says either four minutes of one or five after eleven, I can't make out which, but either way I've been asleep here for over an hour and have missed my five minutes. I lean forward, elbows on knees, head in hands, feeling sick, closing my eyes against the knowledge that it is over, that by relaxing my vigilance, by going to sleep, I have let him die.

Then I hear the sound again—*suck, sigh, swish*—the brief bleep of a heart monitor cut off as the pneumatic doors thump shut, the controlled squeak of rubber-soled shoes, the rhythmic crackle of nylon hampered by static cling.

"You can come in," the nurse says from the doorway. "The doctor's ready for you now."

VII

I walk into the middle of the center unit, hearing the chuff of the tuneless hurdy-gurdies, the bleeps and the sighs and the squeak of soft-soled shoes. His nurse is standing there with the stethoscope still in her ears, frowning. He is as pale as chalk, a man of snow, the hospital gown pulled over him any which way, while the nurse pumps up the bulb frantically, now looking all around the room. "Doctor?" she calls. "Seventy over forty and dropping."

The surgeon looks startled, jumps up from the nurse's station where he has been reading charts, and rushes over, elbowing me aside. He pumps the cuff up himself, jams the stethoscope against the elbow hard. "Oh, Christ, hang two more bags of packed cells *stat*," he orders sharply. "We're losing him."

The nurse runs out and runs back, two bags of dark fluid sloshing in her hands. Another nurse is there now, and they both start trying to poke IV needles into his arms. They poke and poke, again and again.

"Doctor, I can't get a vein," one nurse says quietly.

"Here, give me that," he says, and jams the needle down. I watch as he gets a vein, the dark blood coming down the plastic tube and into the lifted-up vein. He grabs for a foot; the veins are more prominent there, and he quickly stabs another tube and needle in. The patient flushes pink, as though embarrassed, from the feet up. The doctor stands back, nods.

"His color's better already," he says to no one in particular.

"That's a good sign," I say by way of conversation.

Turning, the doctor sees me. "What the fuck is she doing in here?" he demands. "For God's sake get her out."

I stare at the doctor for a moment, then look back down at his face. The eyes are open a narrow shiny slit, his eyeballs like opaque smashed marbles, jerking back and forth as though he's dreaming. And I want to touch him, but as I reach out my hand it wavers, hovers over him outstretched, because with all the tubes and wires and IVs there is not enough clear space to lay it down.

"Hang on," I say to him. "I'm here. Just hang on." As I turn to go, I say to no one in particular, "I'll be in the waiting room next door."

VIII

The surgeon comes in a few minutes later, looking mildly apologetic, to announce that a possibly dangerous situation has developed and "we may have to go back in." But he's going to wait a little while longer, give the situation a chance to correct itself. Meanwhile, he'll be around. He leaves, and standing there in the middle of the waiting room, staring into the closet someone has left open in which mine is now the only coat, I think how nothing ever changes, how this is how it must have been for my father and my mother, my husband and now me. I wish now I had touched him, no matter what. And standing transfixed, rooted to the spot, in my mind I whirl and run headlong away down corridors and hallways of time and space, away from all the hospital rooms and respirators and wires and tubes and nurses and doctors and people who are dying or have died, turn and run, knowing that is exactly what my mother has done before me all those years ago, running away so often in her mind that finally it was her body running too, running away from that unfaceable fact of death, helpless before it, running across the fields away from her children, her friends, her life as well as death, all equally intractable, inscrutable and malevolent. This can't be happening to me, I think; to her, to me, to both of us? I close my eyes and I am running too, down the long corridor, somewhere, anywhere, as long as it's away.

But, rooted to the spot, suddenly I'm aware of my own body separating from that odd kinetic sense of flight. My eyes still closed, I watch the little stick figure diminish in the distance. Why, that's not me, I think, watching the figure grow small. That's not me at all. I'm still here. I'm not you, I say to the small figure. An immense surge of strength sweeps over me; I'm not my mother, I think, I'm myself; I'm different, and I don't have to run. I'm here, I'm me. And suddenly it seems as though I've reached a quiet place where everything is still and calm, and I know I'll be all right no matter what happens. Maybe he will die, but I won't go crazy, because my mother and I are not the same, even if fate has tried to make me think so. I'm staying, and I won't run away. We'll all get through this somehow, whatever comes. But just the same, don't die, I telegraph as hard as I can to the figure in the next room. Don't give up; hang on; don't leave me. Come back, I say to the tiny figure disappearing down the mirror tunnel; come back.

IX

All this time he has in fact been dreaming, and this is his dream:

The two of them are skiing together, their narrow cross-country skis hissing and gliding rhythmically through snow as clean and white and tautly undisturbed as sheets on a newly made bed. He is ahead of her, but he can hear her skis swishing and thumping in unison with his as he strokes the poles forward one after another, strikes and pushes back, his arms working in an easy swinging motion. Kick, swing, glide, kick: faster and faster along the straight and open path, the thump of the skis against the packed snow booming in his ears faster and faster, generating their own momentum, so that in his exhilaration he is short of breath, out of breath, his chest burning, sweat starting to pour off his body, dampening his clothes against his back. Without breaking stride he unzips the front of his windbreaker with one hand, leaving the heavy sweater exposed. Maybe this will cool him off. Behind him he hears her calling.

"Hang on a minute!" she shouts, falling farther and farther behind. He turns to look at her, thinking how purposeful she looks, nead down, all in navy blue, her favorite color, except for the bright red hat. She is stabbing her poles into the snow and coming after him. He thinks how little she has changed in all the years he has known her, that they have been married, and smiles to himself as he thinks of another time in the snow, on the hill behind the library at Cornell, after a big blizzard. Coming upon her in the stacks, her head in a book, he had nudged her.

"Meet you on Libe Slope at three?" She had looked up, startled, and nodded. He still remembers the snow, great drifts of it blown into the hill, the two of them lifting up big chunks and hurling them at each other, he unable even at nearly twice her size to get the better of her, until finally he pushed her into a drift, grabbed her ankles, and dunked her headfirst into a snowbank. He remembers her, face ruddy, streaked with melting snow, snow in her hair and eye-lashes, running over her temples like upside-down tears, laughing and howling "You big bully!", grabbing his leg and pulling on it until he collapsed beside her in a heap of snow. "You give?" But she never gave up, not then, not now. She is coming along now, and he wishes he could wait for her, but something pulls him on, his own momen-tum probably, and he turns his face forward once again, caught up in the rhythm of his own motion. Faster and faster he goes, everything so perfect, until he thinks that he can go no faster. He is almost to the edge of the woods, and it's a good thing, because, all exposed like this, he is begin-ning to feel the cold, and it will be warmer in the woods, not so much wind blowing at him, and he can slow down a little, let it ride. He glances over his shoulder once again to see how far behind she is, and there is just a glimpse of a dark stick figure pressing on far behind him, almost indistinguishable from the first row of trees. He feels slightly puzzled that she is so far back; has he really been going that fast? Still, there is no stopping now. A faint voice floats through the branches, "Don't go so fast, slow down!", but he is too preoccupied now with the wind whistling in his ears, the pounding of his heart and the rushing of blood in his veins, the rasping of his breath, to take notice.

The trees arch over, the smaller ones bent like druids in hoods of snow, the larger ones coming together to form a tunnel barely high enough for his head to clear, the green branches underneath sloping like plumes, the trees closer together now, funneling the wind so that it is as though he is in a subway tunnel, being drawn forward by the wind. The tunnel darkens and the trees grow thicker. He squints ahead, not remembering if he has been this way before. He is shivering now, the cold seeping through and chilling the sweat he has generated in his speed. But he can't stop to rezip his jacket because the path is sloping downhill, and he feels impelled, not merely drawn, toward what appears to be a light warm place at the end of the overarching row of trees. So he goes faster and faster, with only the vaguest memory of her lagging behind and calling to him not to go so fast, and more that he can barely hear. He hopes she won't be angry, think that he has let her down. Still he is headed toward the light now, so fast that it almost seems as though it is not of his own volition, as though he were being sucked or drawn or pushed by the wind all at once, and he is cold, he wishes it were over, and he is out of breath now and his vision is blurred, smearing the tunnel's end, but still he can make out a figure standing at the end of the row of trees. He is curious but cautious and so slows down,

113

takes off his sunglasses even though the light is dazzling.

Uncle Danny? he says, incredulous, for Uncle Danny is standing in the middle of the tunnel, just inside the rim of light, in a bright flowered shirt and a blue polyester leisure suit, a wide grin on his ruddy Irish face. He's silhouetted against the bright light behind him, but it is unmistakably Uncle Danny, whom he has not seen in how many years? But it's not so much the sight of Uncle Danny as the leisure suit that gets him; he's never seen Uncle Danny in one, they weren't that popular when he was alive. Faintly puzzled, he slows up until he is almost at a standstill and approaches Uncle Danny, who, standing casually at the mouth of the tunnel, stretches out a hand in greeting. He starts to stretch a hand out too, so surprised and glad to see Danny after all these years, but before their hands touch, a faint recollection makes him turn to see if she has come into the tunnel yet, if she is still behind him trying to catch up. He shouldn't have gone so far ahead, he thinks, as he searches for her in the long green tunnel full of snow. She is nowhere to be seen. Oh, well, she'll be along, he thinks; it's not as though he has forgotten her completely. Hello, Uncle Danny, he says, stretching out his hand. What are you doing here? Aren't you cold? Uncle Danny doesn't speak but shakes his head and smiles, backs up a step or two, half turning, as he used to when they would go out together, waiting for him to come alongside and walk with him past the rows of houses in Jersey City. Wait a minute, he says to Uncle Danny as he unlocks and steps out of his skis, sticks the poles upright in a pile of snow, where they seem to stick up like cattails, or punks as they called them where he was a boy, gathering them in bundles in the

Jersey meadows. He starts to walk ahead, feeling very cold now, thinking how nice it will be to step into the light. But why is he feeling so cold and exposed, so bare? He looks down and is startled to find that he is stripped down to his swimming trunks, that his skis are nowhere to be seen, that the snow has melted into water frothing white around his ankles. The water lurches forward and starts to roll, making him feel sick to his stomach, and he's confused now, at the voice he hears behind him calling faintly, at the water swirling around his feet, and the loud pounding of the surf growing louder, a roaring in his ears, deafening, so that he can't think, can't move. Uncle Danny is walking just ahead of the rushing water, not too quickly, not urgently, his hands are in his pockets, and he does not urge, but he is waiting for him to catch up and come with him.

I can't come with you now, he hears himself say to Uncle Danny, and he is vaguely surprised because he thought he *was* going; I've got to get back. He has to shout above the roar of the surf, but Uncle Danny smiles and nods, keeps walking on, undisturbed. And as he turns back the waves curl high over his head, rounding into a huge glaucous tunnel of falling water, surrounding him, the skier, the swimmer, as he starts to run back, knee deep in water now, surrounding and engulfing and washing over him, icy cold, so that he chokes and can barely breathe, is gasping as his heart pounds loudly in his ears, and his last recognizable sensation is of being thrown face down in the sand, the breath knocked out of him completely, and rolled and rolled, rocked helplessly back and forth on the beach, cold and wet and out of breath, his mouth full of grit, sand grating on his eyeballs, abrading him everywhere, until all he feels is pain.

The nurse looks up and sees me. "Hi there, Mrs. Boyd," she says cheerfully. "He's awake. Everything's looking pretty good."

He is indeed awake. Behind their slits the saurian glints change color, rotate slowly in my direction. His hand, pressed to his side, flexes briefly, the index finger wiggling. I move closer, rest my cold fingers in his palm. The hand curls up around them; the breath comes hissing, almost inaudible.

"Sara."

"I'm here."

He twists a little, displacing the wires, so that for a moment the tinsel line goes crazy, an earthquake seismograph.

"She's been waiting here the whole time, in and out all night, just to see you," the nurse says. "She thought you were dead."

He turns his head toward me. "I am as you see me," he murmurs. "Ocular proof."

He hears my sharp intake of breath, and his face tightens as though in pain. His breathing quickens to short gasps. The nurse looks concerned, leans toward him anxiously.

"It's a joke," I tell her, my voice shaky.

"No jokes. No tears," he whispers, shutting his eyes. "I hurt." He squeezes my hand hard. "But I'm back."

116

HALLWAYS

When I think of that other time, I think of corridors and hallways, long and reverberative yet muffled, doorways spaced on either side opening into rooms, or other corridors and hallways leading somewhere else. At the far end of the hallway the wall looks blank, but there could be a space on either side. Perhaps the hallway ends, perhaps it only takes another turning. It may be a labyrinth or maze. I can't tell. The nightmare starts when I wake up.

I remember myself as a child, standing with a small mirror poised over my shoulder, trying to see my back in my parents' mirror. The hand-held mirror accidentally catches its own reflection in the other mirror and opens suddenly into a tunnel winding down and through, an infinite series of diminishing rims of hand-held mirrors reflecting back

117

and forth. I stand in the middle, paralyzed, staring at the tunnel stretching forward, stretching back.

I stand and look. Where I am now is not a tunnel; it's a hospital corridor, one I move down with familiarity, if not with ease. I know where I am. Still there is a trick of perspective. As I walk down these hallways, I often feel this surge of strangeness, this rounding of the corridor into a tunnel winding down. The farther away they are, the closer the doors seem until there is one after another with no space in between. Behind any of these doors may be a way out, upward into light or safety or simply somewhere else. But as my mind flies down the tunnel, there is no time to think whether to open one or keep straight on. The end of the tunnel is where we're going, and all the doors are closed.

We walk down the corridor side by side, Sam and I, peering into doorways to see if there's a vacant room where we can talk. All the waiting rooms are crowded, televisions blaring, people talking, killing time.

"This way," he says, lightly touching my arm. "I know a place." A moment later we are in the small waiting room next to the intensive care unit. The lights are out; the room is empty. "Slow day," he says as he sits down. I hesitate in the doorway. I've been here before, and not on a slow day.

Looking mildly abstracted, he begins to rummage in the pockets of his lab coat. Out of one pocket he drags a pipe, the other a tobacco pouch. He sits back, crosses his legs, and begins to fill his pipe.

"So Phil is dying," I say from the doorway.

Sam looks up startled. After all, he hasn't said so in so many words. After a brief hesitation, he nods. "That's right."

"How long?"

Sam clears his throat, squints up at the ceiling while his fingers continue to push tobacco into the pipe bowl. "That depends," he says finally.

"A year?"

"Not that long."

"Six months?"

"Maybe." The lighter glares, and he sucks in the smoke, holds it, puffs it out.

I go over to the couch across from him. The cushions wheeze heavily as I sit down.

"Will he be in pain?" I ask finally.

"No, not what you'd call real pain. Discomfort is a better word."

I look at him, thinking how odd that phrase sounds, that really there are no better words. I let my head fall back and watch the smoke whirl toward the air vent high on the wall.

"What will it be like?"

Sam sucks his pipe, blows smoke, considering. "The tumor will grow and fill up space, press on other organs, blood vessels. There will be edema. Toward the end he won't be able to walk. . . ."

"Will his mind be clear?" My voice sounds oddly small and far away, attenuated, like the smoke.

He nods. "Unless it spreads to his brain. I doubt it; it doesn't seem to be that kind of tumor. And there probably won't be time."

I'm starting to feel drowsy, dopey, probably the effect of

watching the smoke swirl away, and of course I haven't been sleeping well the last few nights since Phil was admitted, while they were running all the tests. I find myself thinking of the room next door, where Phil was for so long after the operation, and then again when he hemorrhaged. Before that, I could never imagine what it had been like for my father, but now I can, with the tubes and the oxygen and the heart monitor, and the nurses' shoes squeaking hurriedly, the doctors whispering and shaking their heads. I can imagine myself there with Phil again.

"This is better," I say after a moment.

"What?" He blinks at me in disbelief, a lit match poised over his pipe, his ministrations momentarily arrested.

"I was thinking about my father. He died suddenly. This is better. This way there'll be time to get ready, time to say goodbye."

A ragged noise splits the air as Sam clears his throat again. He ought to get that taken care of, I think absently. I watch him as he shifts in his chair. The smoke shifts too, as though it were a part of him.

"Oh." He looks at me skeptically, then nods. We sit quietly for a minute or so. Then he says, "What do you think he'll want to do?"

"About what?"

He looks momentarily annoyed, probably by my apparent lack of attention; he likes to get these discussions over with. Not only that, his pipe has gone out. He takes it out of his mouth, stares at it in disgust. "How do you think he'll want to go? There are things we can do to prolong life. Take out the remaining kidney and put him on dialysis." Sam pauses; the discovery two days ago during one of the first tests that Phil has only one kidney left has caused some consternation around here, to put it mildly. No one seems to know what happened to it; either it was destroyed during the big bleed ten days after the operation—Sam's theory—or it was removed by mistake during the operation. Anyway, as Sam said earlier, that's the least of our worries. Or is it?

Sam clears his throat again and goes on. "Then we could remove bulk tumor, buy some time. Maybe years."

I stare at him. Time for what?

"What kind of time is another question," he says. He peers at the inside of his pipe as if bewildered by the failure of smoke, then takes out a penknife and begins to poke at it. The penknife makes a hollow, abrasive sound, like painful breathing. "If it were me," he says finally, "I would do nothing."

He looks up at me, pausing in his vigorous scraping of the pipe bowl. Abruptly he stands up, moves to the doorway, looks back at me over his shoulder.

"If he asks me, that's what I'm going to tell him." He walks out without another word.

I jump up and run over to the door, peer down the hall at his shrinking figure. Hey, wait a minute, I start to call out, but he's too far away, his stocky, white-coated figure duck-walking swiftly toward the other end. Then I realize I'm angry. "Why, you bastard," I mutter to his back. "Don't you dare. What the hell do you know?" But I don't run after him to tell him that. It's too late; he's turned a corner out of sight.

The nurses have given special permission for the kids to visit, so in the evening I bring Linnie to see Phil. It's easier to bring each child alone; together they are so restless and inquisitive and nervous, constantly interrupting, asking for money for the candy machine, the coffee shop, never settling down to visit. It is impossible for their father and me to carry on a conversation, and once here they do not seem interested in talking or even looking at this strange pale daddy who has to lie flat in his bed so his blood pressure won't rise any more beyond its present sufficiently dangerous level, or go so low that he'll pass out the way he did in the bathroom the other morning. They can't stop for a second. And yet they always want to come.

Tonight David is at a friend's for supper, so Linnie and I have come alone. She spends some time sitting next to Phil on the bed, but after a while she gets restless.

"Mom, can I go to the coffee shop?"

She is so little, only eight. But it will give us some time to talk alone. "Do you know the way?" I ask.

She looks insulted. "Of course. I'm not a baby anymore. David and I have been there lots of times." I give her a quarter and she leaves, small legs moving briskly, all business, proud of not being a baby anymore. I turn back to Phil as soon as she is out of sight; we can use this time to get some things straightened out.

Probably half an hour goes by before we realize that she has not come back. "Where do you suppose Linnie is?" Phil asks suddenly.

I stand up and glance around the room. "She's not back yet?" The stark realization is that we haven't even missed her; we've been too preoccupied. "Damn. She must have gotten lost. I'll have to go look for her."

Phil's not supposed to get out of bed, but he throws back the covers. I shake my head, replace them. "It's all right, I'll find her. I'll be back," I say as I leave the room.

I walk down the corridor. It's a small hospital, only three floors, two wings, in the shape of an H. But the wings are long, and all the turnings look the same. There are doorways on every side, some open, some closed. Whispers and hissings and bubblings of strange machines drift out into the hallway, odd gurglings and snorings, a cough, a choke, a moan. I try to imagine how it must be for a child. She has been here before, she has even been here often. She knows the way, wants to go alone. "I'm not a baby anymore." The noises grow louder, whispers, hissings, the hush of a door closing; the throat clearings and retchings mount and fill the corridor with a din that shrinks me to her size, and I feel a sudden urge to run, even to hide. But running in a hospital suggests a medical emergency, Code Red, and this is only a lost little girl.

I go straight to the elevator. Fascinated by technology, of course she would take the elevator, push the button herself and go down; she and her brother have done it many times. It is only recently that she has been able to reach it; now she does it every chance she gets, fighting David for the privilege. "No, let me." I step into the elevator, trying to imagine myself in her place, and press the button marked 1. The elevator whooshes shut and lurches down a floor.

More corridors, more doors, offices this time, all empty, doors all locked. I turn the corner halfway down and walk quickly to the coffee shop.

"Have you seen my little girl?" The woman behind the counter is not the usual one; she doesn't know me.

"How little?"

"She's about this high, light brown hair, brown eyes, wearing . . ." I can't remember what she is wearing. The woman behind the counter looks at me with disapproval. How could I lose a little girl in a place like this and not even remember what she's wearing? Why would I bring her here in the first place?

"Is she a patient?"

"No, oh, no. We're just visiting her father."

The woman gestures toward the magazine rack. "There was a little girl over there looking at comics. But that was a while ago. She bought some gum and left."

"Did you see which way . . . ?"

"Sorry." She turns away; the coffee shop is closing for the night. She doesn't seem particularly concerned or even interested, let alone sympathetic. She probably blames me for losing my little girl, for being careless and letting her out of my sight. I should know better in a place like this. Just then a voice over the intercom says pleasantly, "Visiting hours are now over. Visiting hours are now over. Thank you." I go out the door and down the hall, back the way I came.

And of course I find her. She has gone straight on instead of turning left, taken the wrong elevator—they all look alike—pressed the button for 2, and come out in another country.

She is huddled in the angle of the floor and the wall in the middle of a corridor that opens off the one Phil's room is on. She has been so close all the time, just around the corner, just out of sight. It was only a question of finding the right hallway. As I walk toward her, I can see she has been crying; her cheeks are blotched and streaked, her eyes are swollen. But she is not crying now; she's staring straight ahead, her eyes glazed and hopeless. The only indication of how long she's been crying is the slight rhythmic catch that jerks her rib cage, the trembling of her body as she takes a breath. She is so quiet I can see why no one has noticed her. I have told her and her brother many times that they must be quiet, they must not bother anyone, or the nurses won't let them come. And of course she could be anybody's child, sent outside to sit in the hall while Mommy and Daddy say goodbye for the night. I walk up and stand next to her, and still she does not see me.

"Linnie."

She looks up, startled, takes one long shuddering breath, and bursts into tears. I kneel down, put my arms around her, pick her up, and hold her as she twines her arms and legs around me the way she did when she was smaller, buries her head in my shoulder.

"I guess you got lost, huh?"

She nods her head in the hollow of my shoulder, her breath still catching. I begin to walk with her down the hall toward the turning that will take us back to Phil's room.

"But I knew that you were lost and I found you, didn't I?"

Again the little head nods and she sighs, her body losing some of its stiffness. She relaxes against me, and for a moment reminds me of the tiny infant she once was, so closely fitted to my body, needing me and nothing else but air. The sobs subside, then stop.

Partway down the hall she stiffens again and starts to wriggle downward. "Let me down. I want to walk." I let her slither down, but I still hold her hand. The first steps are interrupted by her hiccups, but soon they too subside.

"Don't tell Daddy I got lost," she says as we walk along. I look down at her; she's blinking and wiping her eyes and drying her face. She doesn't want Phil to know or see that she's been crying. Already she carries with her a sensitivity about causing other people pain, feels guilty for not behaving well. She doesn't want Daddy to know, doesn't want him to think badly of her.

"I won't," I say. I can't bring myself to tell her he already knows. But he will not be angry or upset when we get there; he will smile and say casually, "Hi there, where've you been?" and that will be that.

Later on that night, after we've come home and everyone is asleep, Linnie wakes in the night. I hear her calling to me. I hurry to her room and she is sitting on her bed, in the angle of the wall and the mattress, her eyes wide and terrified. She's so shocked she isn't even crying. She reaches out and grabs my arm, pulls me toward her like a drowning person hauling on a rope. "I dreamed that robbers came and took me away, and I got away from them, but I didn't know where I was and you didn't know where I was, and I couldn't get back to you." She shuts her eyes and bursts into racking sobs, twisting and clutching the sleeve of my nightgown in her hands.

I lie down, pulling her next to me, settling her head into the crook of my arm, and cuddle her body into mine again. As I stroke her hair, I say, "If you were lost, wherever you were in the whole wide world, I would find you. I would look and look and look and never stop until we were together again."

"But what if you didn't know I was lost? What if you thought I had just left on purpose?"

"How could I not know that you were lost? I knew you were lost at the hospital, didn't I? And that time you got off the school bus at the wrong stop I knew right away and came and found you?"

"Uh huh. But it was long."

"But I still found you. It seemed long, but it wasn't, and I found you, and now we're together again."

"Uh huh." She sighs, pops her thumb in her mouth, and smiles, her eyes closing. "I'll never leave you," she says. Then she turns away on her side, her head rolling off my arm, and goes back to sleep.

I lie there for a long while, feeling the sweaty warmth of her little girl's body. I think about what I've said to her, and realize I've repeated almost word for word what I said to Phil the afternoon his doctor told us he was dying. Now I remember sitting next to him on the bed after Sam had left, watching his face.

"I don't really think that I'm afraid of death, not anymore. But I feel so bad for the rest of you." His eyes glaze over but he doesn't blink, just stares at me. "This is the worst thing I could have done to you," he finally whispers.

I know that he is thinking about my father's death, so long ago now. I was twelve, my sister and brother six and almost five. David is barely eleven, and Linnie is only eight.

"I just don't want to leave you," he says finally, and then he shuts his eyes. The tears spill out gently, seep into the hollows around his nose, along his ears, catch on the pinpoint stubble of his beard. I wipe them with both hands, tracing the lines and hollows with my thumbs.

Trying to think of something to say that might comfort him, comfort both of us, I put my hands on his shoulders while my mind whirls away through emptiness, searching for the words. "You know how I've carried my father all these years." He nods. "I'll take you with me just the way I have my father. You will be with me. You'll be with all of us."

He shakes his head slightly. "But you won't be there, and I won't be here. We'll be in different countries."

"You don't know that. Nobody knows that. Remember your dream the other time? If there's a way to find you, I'll find you. Wherever you are in that other country, I'll find you. I don't care how big it is. I'll look and look and never stop until we're together again."

It's enough. He stares up at me for a long moment, then sighs and shuts his eyes again, settles back on the pillow. He smiles, and his body relaxes slightly. I let out the breath I have been holding, carefully, so that it will not sound like a sigh. "And meanwhile I'll carry you with me. We all will."

"I hope so," he says. I put my cheek next to his, lean myself against his chest, wrap my arms around his shoulders as far as they will go. He puts his arms around me. Our cheeks slide back and forth a little, slippery with tears. It's an odd sensation, and I feel the muscles of Phil's cheek bunch into a smile. I smile too. I'm thinking of him, of what I've just said, and I'm thinking of my father, dead these twenty-eight years, and how a part of me has been look-ing for him all this time, still hoping there'd been some mistake.

But I know, have always known, that I was searching in the wrong place, that no power of will or reason could pene-trate that barrier of time and space that separates us. He's in a place I'm not, a place that I can't get to with my reason or my will, or even with my love. It's only in a dream that I still believe that I might find him. If he were only lost, I would have found him. If love could save, I would have saved him. And yet he's with me, just as I have said. In a way he's never left. So what I've said to Phil is true; I have carried my father with me all these years, as real a presence in my life as those who are alive but in some other place.

As I sit up and wipe my eyes, I look at Phil and see the lines of pain erased. Somehow I've said the right thing, at least for now. And I too feel relieved.

After I've left Linnie and gone back to my own bed, I think about my words to her, to Phil. "If you were lost, wherever you were, I would look and look and never stop until I found you and we were together again." And I realize that this is not an expression of power, or certainty, or even of belief, but only of my own determination never to give up, never to let go. I might look and look, that much is in my power, but who is to say that I would ever find? And to them the wait-ing would seem long.

THE DEATH OF THE DOG
AND OTHER RESCUES

It's a typical Saturday morning in October. Linnie's due at a birthday party at noon, but I've rushed into town with both kids to get sneakers, and we're late so I'm feeling pressed and a little cross at David, who had a fit in the shoe store because he couldn't find new sneakers that looked and felt exactly like his old ones; and I'm worried about the three other little girls I'm supposed to pick up, waiting all dressed up wondering what happened to us, and the little girl whose party it is thinking no one is going to come, so as I turn into the driveway I say over my shoulder to Linnie, "Now as soon as I stop the car you jump right out, run in, and get dressed as fast as you can, because we're late."

"I don't want to be late," she wails, tears jumping out of her eyes.

131

"Well, it's too late not to be late now, so just do it," I answer sharply. David is scrunched down in the back seat glaring at me in the rearview mirror, elbows jammed down on the new sneakers box with the old sneakers inside, not talking.

Phil looks up, smiling. He's out in his shorts mowing the lawn for what he fervently hopes is the last time of this long Indian summer we got in trade for the real summer that never came. It's so warm he's not wearing a shirt; he's finally gotten over his self-consciousness about the big scar from his operation, and his whole upper body is tan and greased with sweat, the scar looping up from his shorts and across his ribs with a little jog at the end like an upside-down hockey stick. The truth is, it's barely noticeable now, especially when he's tan. The dog is lying beside the driveway panting slightly in the heat; he bumps his tail on the ground as our wheels crunch down the driveway. He can't hear us because he's deaf now, but he feels our vibrations and turns his head in our direction as we pass, tail gyrating wildly. He's very old, fifteen, in fact, but the same foxy bright-eyed collie face he had as a young dog looks up expectantly to see who's here. Even now in his old age he is in truth a handsome dog, a rake, a pirate, an Errol Flynn of a dog. We've had him all our married life and even before, ever since he was a puppy almost too young to stand on all fours, his back legs not quite strong enough to hold up his rear end.

Phil waves briefly, cantilevers the mower around, and starts back down the grass. He's left the gas can and funnel at the edge of the driveway not far from the dog, who is also at the edge just off the grass, out of the way of the mower.

As I yank on the brake and hop out of the car to open the kids' door I think how peaceful it all is, what a nice day we have here, and isn't everything going well?

But there's the party, and we're late. "Come on, Linnie, let's step on it. Crying doesn't get you anywhere."

"I don't know where the present is." She sniffles. I hold the back door open with one hand over her head to let her pass.

"I hate my new sneakers," David mutters, ducking under my arm. He has an additional grievance. "I want to go too. I never get to go anywhere."

"You weren't invited," I say from the middle of the cupboard where I've stashed the present for the birthday girl.

"Mom! Mom!" Linnie screams hysterically from upstairs. "I need you!"

"Just for the ride," David says glumly as I run upstairs to Linnie.

Inside of three minutes we are all running back out to the car. The doors slam, one, two, three, the motor roars, the radio blares, the kids are squabbling and I can't hear a thing, can't even think, and I jam the car into reverse and back up fast, bump, crunch, right over some hard but hollow object that crumples under my wheels. "What's that! What's that?" the kids holler, peering all around, and I look up through the windshield to see Phil, a horrified look on his face, waving frantically at me, gesticulating wildly as though we were in some terrible imminent danger. He's shouting at me, but the windows are rolled up and the radio is blaring and the kids are yammering so loud I can't hear him, so I try to read his lips as he pantomimes disaster, something about the door, but all the doors are shut, I heard them, and then I realize I must have run over the loaded gas can and we are going to catch fire and explode so, always quick to respond to danger, I shove the gear into forward and pull ahead crunch, crunch, buckle, away from the ruined gas can and the leaking gas so we won't explode, pull forward out of danger and turn off the ignition so we're safe. No one can say I don't react well in a crisis.

But Phil has really gone crazy now, dancing and whirling and hopping up and down, bending forward with his hands over his stomach as though he were going to throw up, then standing up with his eyes closed and flinging one arm out as if were throwing a Frisbee in a gesture of what I take to be despair, and I watch him, puzzled, because haven't I done the right thing?

But of course not, because it's not the gas can that has gotten up, moved and flopped its old arthritic bones down in a heap behind the car where I never thought to look. It's not the gas can I have run over, crunching and crumpling it not once but twice, coming and going this bright fall day—it's the dog.

II

He was always a handsome dog. This line, a joke between Phil and me because it was so literally true, has for some reason always reminded me of my father. There is a photograph of the dog in his younger days lying on the lawn in what we always called his noble-dog pose, nose lifted, eyes staring off in the distance, a faintly ironic, tolerant, ever-so-slightly self-conscious expression on his face. There is a similar photograph of my father when he was very young and very handsome, dressed to the nines in white shark-skin coat and knickers, sitting in a lawn chair with his legs crossed, cigarette dangling casually from his fingers. He looks wonderful, one eyebrow cocked wittily, like a blond Robert Taylor without the mustache. Someone has just said to him, "Jim, you are a handsome dog," and he is regarding that person with a tolerant, amused, ironic smile as if to say, Yes, I know, but it doesn't really matter, that's just the way I am.

When Phil and I were first married and had no children, the dog went everywhere with us. People would stop us on the street and say, "Oh, what a pretty dog!" then mystify us by asking "Is he ugly?" and when we shook our heads, be-wildered, not understanding at first that they meant his temper, not his beauty, they'd reach down to stroke his white ruff, his blond fur, scratch behind his foxy ears, ad-mire his dainty paws. Cars would slow down, children across the street would tug at their mothers' sleeves and call out, "Look, a little Lassie! A little Lassie, see?" Actually he was not a little Lassie at all, except for his color and markings not even close. In fact he was a collie-shepherd mix with big limpid brown eyes and a wedge-shaped shep-herd nose, pointy upright ears, and long but not really shaggy fur. But some genetic accident had made him look, as so seldom happens with mixed-breed dogs, as though he had got that way on purpose. We always thought he was a throwback to those first small wiry blunt-nose mountain collies before they were bred up to size with coats like llamas, torpedo noses, and beady little snake eyes on the sides of their heads. Because he was a crossbreed, we knew that there would never be another one quite like him.

Even if he fathered puppies, which in his green and salad days running loose he certainly must have, he would not breed true.

We got him unexpectedly when he was very small, his whole litter abandoned in Phil's sister's dorm at college, brought home while we were visiting and given the bum's rush from Phil's mother's kitchen right into our car for the trip back up to school. And there he stayed for all our travels, at first so little he curled up under the seat with only his wedge-shaped nose sticking out in front; then, as he grew bigger, under my feet in the front footwell where as a grown dog he just fit and felt secure. In a paroxysm of graduate school cuteness we named him Collie Cibber after the eighteenth-century poet laureate and enemy of Pope, and in some ways he lived up to his name. He was a fop, a dandy, the only dog I've ever seen licking his fine white paws clean and then polishing his face just like a cat. He went everywhere with us, was well known, even legendary, on campus for herding students into our classes, nipping officiously at their ankles, rounding them up and ushering them through the door, then thumping down with a resigned and drawn-out groan across the doorway, stretching out on his back with his legs sticking up, underbelly exposed, and ostentatiously going off to sleep, punctuating my lectures with an occasional snore. When the bell rang at the end of class he invariably leaped bolt upright, startled and sleepy-faced, abashed, then recovered himself, shook down his fur, and stood sentry by the door as the students filed out. For years after the children came, first David, then Linnie, he refused to acknowledge their existence, would never come when they called or lift a paw to shake

their hands as he did ours, suffered by no means gladly
their mawlings and pettings. He was our first and in his
eyes remained our only child, was one of us, never seeming
to take in the fact that he was much the furriest and generally though not always ate and slept on the floor. And he
was perfect, charming, bright, intelligent, yes, a handsome dog.

III

Ever since my father died suddenly away from home when
I was twelve, I have felt that it was my responsibility to keep
everyone around me safe. This has meant saving them
when necessary, at the very least hovering somewhat officiously, a walking first-aid manual, rapid extricator and
rehabilitator of lost causes. Phil has called this my rescuer
complex, but, complex or not, I can't help believing deep
down that whatever is lost can be recovered, what is broken
can be mended, and what is gone replaced; at least it's
worth a try. So over the years I have tracked down within
minutes children missing from the school bus at the ap-
pointed stop, yanked out drowning ones before they could
inhale a single drop of water, righted capsized sailboats,
glued back together broken objects, recovered a single
dropped earring of little real but great sentimental value
from the middle of a well-used tennis court. Quick off the
blocks, I have rescued no later than the third thump
around the dryer a cat suicidally fond of sleeping in odd
places. I have toughed it out with barely a murmur in
countless waiting areas, emergency rooms, ICUs, stood
close and watchful while my husband struggled through

the numerous nearly fatal complications of a botched and messy operation for a tumor the size of a dumbbell in his belly, clutching his hand and muttering "Don't leave me" while I nagged the doctors with questions gleaned from medical textbooks—What does this mean? Have you checked that? What happens next, and are you positively absolutely sure?—determined not to lose him the way we did my father. Now I, who have weathered any number of these crises and near-misses without losing control, I, the cool, the calm, the take-charge person, leap screeching out of the car with my two hands simultaneously trying to cover my eyes, my ears, my mouth, run screaming hysterically into the house and up the stairs as fast and as far away as I can get, howling at the top of my lungs, "Oh, no, dear God, not the dog, please, not the goddamned dog!" In my carelessness and haste, I, the rescuer, the caretaker, have run over and killed my own dog.

I finally skid to a halt upstairs in the bedroom that overlooks the driveway. I creep over to the window, cautiously uncovering one eye, ready to leap back if it's too awful, and take a look.

Phil is bending over the dog, who is lying in some sort of heap in the middle of the driveway. Then Phil takes a step back and I stare in disbelief. The dog is not dead after all.

In fact, he is sprawled more or less upright in a version of his stately noble-dog pose, swinging his head around and looking a little dazed, obviously trying to figure out what hit him. He looks pretty much the same, and I can't quite believe it; can it be we've both been spared? Then I notice his hindquarters aren't quite right; they are askew and slightly flattened, one leg sticking out behind at an awkward angle.

No, he has definitely been run over. I watch, holding my breath, expecting him to expire before my eyes, while Phil reaches forward. The dog sniffs at his hand, his tail starts to twitch, then gyrate slightly, whisking up a little cloud of gravel. He is wagging his tail. Wow, I think, that's a good sign, his tail still works, his spine must not be crushed. In the back of the car the children gaze in fascinated horror, their noses pressed against the rear window. I go into the bathroom and throw up.

But the dog is still alive. I have not killed him, at least not so far. He's hurt, of course, but what is broken can be mended. I splash water on my face and go downstairs, sidle over to the car; I still can't go near the dog. I yell to Phil that I'm going to take the kids on up to the Lanes' and to the party, that he should call the vet. As I back around past him he shakes his head as though to say, Don't get your hopes up. On the way up the road I consider the probability that, even though he is not dead, the dog is so badly hurt he'll have to be put to sleep when we take him into the vet's. How many dogs can get run over and survive? So this re-prieve is only temporary; the reckoning comes soon.

When I arrive at the Lanes' house I am in a terrible state. The three little girls are lined up beside the driveway with their presents clutched to their smocked bosoms, looking anxious. I can hardly talk, but Joyce just nods; Phil has called ahead with the news. She is sympathetic; once she ran over a kitten, which proceeded to get up, shake itself, and dance loosely toward her with its crushed bones, then leaped straight into the air and died at her feet. She felt terrible for weeks, still dreams of it sometimes. "Come on, shove over," she says. "I'll drive."

Everyone piles into the car, and we drive back down the road and stop at the top of our driveway. I get out and she pulls away in the direction of the birthday party, but not before I hear Katie's shrill voice: "Did Sara really squash Cibber flatter than a pancake?" I walk down the drive, forgetting that with the car gone we have no way to transport the dog to the vet's eleven miles away.

The dog is still alive, breathing fast and whimpering, one leg stuck out behind at that funny angle, otherwise apparently intact, if a little flat. There is no blood, no splintered bone. "Sorry, old man, I didn't mean to," I say as I walk over to him. He does not bump his tail this time, only blinks up at me desperately, his breath rasping. Oh, oh, I think, progressive trauma; we're losing him. We've got to do something. I bend down and put a hand out toward him.

"Don't touch him," Phil says quickly. I look up to see that he is holding a towel to his neck, and there is blood congealing on his bare shoulder. He shrugs. "I wanted to get him away before you came back so you wouldn't have to see him, but when I tried to pick him up he whipped right around and bit me on the neck." He takes the towel away and I see the two deep toothmarks oozing blood, no more than an inch from Phil's carotid artery. "Do you fucking believe it?" Phil says by way of conversation. I shake my head; I fucking don't. I look back down at the dog, who is making impatient wheeping noises like faint radar bleeps as if to say, Well, don't just stand there, do something. He peers around at his rear end and his front paws contract as he digs into the gravel, trying to stand up. Old as he is, this is not easy in the best of circumstances, and now it is clearly impossible. He shifts his front paws, gazes up faintly puzzled at the two of us, and groans.

"I'll get a blanket," I tell Phil, and run into the house, thinking about first aid for shock and keeping the victim warm.

"Do you think we can move him?" I ask Phil after I've covered the dog up.

"We'll have to," Phil says. "The vet can't make house calls; the trauma truck is in the shop. Besides, they don't come out this far."

So we have to drive the dog into town, but that's all right, because Phil will have to go to the emergency room anyway to get his neck sewed up. We need a car, and ours is gone to the birthday party. Just then our neighbor down the street arrives with his son. They have heard my screams and want to know if they can help. He and Phil and the son confer over the dog's head about what to do, and because they seem able to take care of everything, I wander back inside, out of earshot. But I watch out the window while the three of them tie the dog's mouth shut with an old nylon stocking, arrange him on a blanket sling, and hoist him into the back of our neighbor's brand-new Volvo station wagon. I peer out the window until they're out of sight, and when Joyce arrives with the car I drop her and David at her house and follow the others into town.

IV

And after all that, the dog is not only not dead, according to the vet he is not even dying, or in immediate danger of it.

The vet on call, a short stocky woman with small hands, tells me there are no other contiguous eight inches of dog I could have run over without killing him outright. I have run over the pelvic arch, breaking it in three places, and there may be some kidney and bladder damage, some nerve and muscle bruising, but it's not too bad, considering. A close call, she says, and of course his age will be a factor in recovery, but they'll keep him under sedation and quiet for a few days until the bones can set—you can't put a cast on a dog's ass, or anyone else's, for that matter—and then we can take him home and go from there. So things are clearly not as bad as we first thought. "You're a lucky dog," she says as she gathers up the dog, his nose still tied shut, and starts out back with him. "You'd better get that seen to," she says casually over her shoulder to Phil, "before you bleed to death." Phil blinks and goes pale; he is no stranger to the possibility of bleeding to death. But of course she's only kidding. "Call us tomorrow," she shouts from the back room. "We'll probably know better then." And that's it; she and the dog are gone.

Phil and I stand there, flabbergasted. I can't believe it. A fifteen-year-old dog run over and squashed flat, and we can pick him up in a few days? It seems incredible, too good to be true, but naturally I'm relieved. Still, after our trip to the emergency room—five stitches, not a record, only average for us—as we drive home in the dark I prepare myself for the worst. The dog may not recover, he may not walk again, life may not be worth living to him as an invalid, a cripple. Phil has always been more adamant on this issue than I, especially since his illness; he is a confirmed quality-of-lifer. So I try to face up to the fact that we may finally have to make a decision we have been dreading these last few years as the dog has grown more stiff and feeble, the time when—if he did not die a sudden and natural death the way my first dog Barney did at fourteen, his age and mine, conveniently expiring in seconds on the living room rug— we would have to say the word and have him put to sleep. I have contemplated this and decided I would want to be there to see him out, the good old friend. The vet has not said anything about putting the dog to sleep, not even as a remote possibility, but just in case, I say to Phil as we drive along, "He's had a good life, at least there's that. He's been a happy dog. So if it *does* come to that it's not so bad." I hear a sniffle next to me, and look over to see the tears rolling down Phil's cheeks, along his jaw, and into the gauze bandage. Choked up but dry-eyed—lately I seem to have lost the knack of tears—I say, "Come on, you know, he's really just a dog." Phil nods, but I can tell it doesn't help one bit.

V

Still, rescued for the moment from the worst consequences of my own haste and negligence, I ponder this latest in a long series of other such near-misses and close calls, so many, in fact, that I have come to think of myself as some sort of lightning rod for disasters that don't quite happen, or turn out at the last moment not to be so bad. We are certainly no strangers to the odd laceration, the quick and bloody trip to the emergency room with thumbs held over pressure points, towels and ice packs pressed to rapidly rising lumps and contusions. Oddly enough, these stitches of Phil's are his first, not counting the ones from his operation. David at age ten has had his head split open twice, has put his hand through the glass storm door, cutting it badly in three places, and nearly taken the top of his thumb off within minutes of acquiring his new Swiss army knife. I am in second place with the scar—now barely visible—over my eyebrow from falling into the garbage can when I stepped on one of David's toy trucks, and Linnie is a distant fourth with two tiny stitches on the bridge of her nose where David whacked her accidentally last winter with the snow shovel. These are the near-misses—the eye not put out, the artery not sliced, the tendon unsevered—dreadful possibilities that you never think of until after it's all over, and you just wipe your brow and sigh deeply with relief that it wasn't worse. Even more unsettling are the close calls, those terrible calamities that somehow are revoked after you have accepted the reality of their happening, fully entered into the altered state of post-disaster conscious-ness, the ones that give you that strange sense of dissocia-tion, as though you might be dreaming that they didn't happen because they are so awful, but in a little while you will wake up and find they have. So the children do *not* roll out and get smashed dead at 60 miles an hour through the back door of the station wagon I have carelessly left un-latched in my hurry to get somewhere. Thanks to a friend with quick reflexes who grabs her arm before she can pull it back through, Linnie does *not* lacerate and scar her hand for life after putting it through the other glass storm door panel we have not had the sense to replace after David's accident. And the tender skin at the back of David's knee is *not* after all impaled on the rusty barbed-wire fence six miles from help as in our panic we at first believed, but only pinched between two prongs, the skin hardly even broken, and even though after I have freed him he falls over in a dead faint from sheer fright, he recovers almost immediately.

So the dog run over but not killed is only the latest in a long list of these bizarre remissions, close calls, near-misses, lost causes not so lost after all. And I wonder sometimes what I have done to deserve this peculiar brand of good fortune, or if in fact it is a kind of test, a punishment, to be always coming up short of real disaster, always running to the rescue, always compelled to see what I can do. And do I keep at it because it somehow seems to work?

On the kitchen table among the other odds and ends I find this note printed in my daughter's hand. It's the beginning of a story she has to write for school. "A mother is telling her daughter to keep trying and not to give." That's as far as she's gotten, but it makes me wonder if I have done my children any favors by instilling—not only that but apparently demonstrating—this attitude of "keep trying and not to give." Whatever is broken can be mended, whatever is lost can be replaced, whatever is missing can be found, whatever is sick can be healed. It's all done with mirrors after all, and there's no such word as can't. But, I often wonder, by jumping on my horse and riding in all directions, usually to some, if not complete, avail, have I given them an impression of life that is not really true? How will they know, if and when the time comes, how to give? How will I? Sometimes in my worst daydreams I imagine a plane crash or shipwreck in the middle of a dark cold ocean, the four of us floating survivors with no hope of rescue, or a nuclear bomb blast not too near but near enough, so that it's just a matter of time before the death cloud hits. I imagine them clinging to me, looking at me, asking "What are we going to do?" And for once there will be nothing, absolutely nothing, I can do.

VI

Four days after the accident I go to pick up the dog. Our regular vet is there, the one who's taken care of the dog all these years. He's kind but not a sentimentalist, and when he sees me he just shakes his head. "I was sorry to hear what happened; I know how crazy you are about that dog."

"He's a good old friend," I say in a slightly choked-up voice. But I don't cry. After all, it's just a dog, and there are worse things than running over your own dog, particularly if the dog survives.

The vet brings the dog out, his mouth tied shut with a strap, puts him in the back of the car for me. The dog's eyes look wild and desperate; he growls at the vet, nudges him sharply with his tied-up nose; if it weren't the strap he'd bite him for sure. "You'll have to tie his jaw shut whenever you move him," the vet says. "He's pretty strong for an old dog, and he sure knows how to use those teeth." He slams the door shut. "Give me a call in about a week, let me know how he's doing," he says through the window, then adds ominously, "if he's making any progress." That's it; I drive home with the dog.

The kids and Phil have set up a bed in the kitchen, a camp mattress, David's old sleeping bag, the smelly blanket the dog sometimes curls up on, and newspapers all over. The red plastic dog dish and a ceramic bowl for water—

over the years he has become accustomed to drinking from the toilet bowl, but that's out of range for the time being— are neatly arranged at one end of the bed. I lug the dog in, protesting through his tied-up teeth, and lay him down, untie the strap from his nose. He just lies there panting, his head and chest erect, front pawls parallel, looking from one of us to the other. He whimpers a little, then groans, staring up at me. But there is no way, I tell myself, that he could know I did it, just a sudden dark shadow, a heavy crushing weight, and pain. No, he couldn't know. But just the same I'll make it up to you, old man, I promise silently. I will make you better; I will make you well.

As it turns out, it's just as well I've made this solemn vow, because the dog will not let anyone else come near him, even to tie up his mouth. He growls and snaps at Phil and the kids if they so much as put a hand out. He will not let me pick him up with his mouth untied. Clearly unable to help himself, he snaps at me and then sinks his head down sheepishly, apologetic. He submits, blinking in humiliation, when I come toward him with the nylon stocking, but lets me tie it around his nose and behind his ears, so I can pick him up.

At first he cries all night. For a while I sit with him, but I keep falling asleep in the chair, so I go upstairs and collapse into a stupor, in which I still hear him yelping and moaning faintly throughout the night. In the morning I find him at one end of his bed, as far as he can get from the puddles and piles of dog shit, looking up at me with that bright foxy look, shifting his front paws in restless expectation as though to say, Let's get on with it.

And get on with it we do. I learn to recognize a certain

tone of whimper and restless scrabbling as a signal he wants to go out, so I tie his mouth, hoist him up—for an old arthritic bony dog he's still no lightweight—take him outside, where he does his business lying down. There are accidents, but fewer and fewer as we get our signals straight, and picking him up seems to hurt him less and less. He does not complain much, eats and slurps up water, and watches us all go in and out, following us with the old bright foxy look, still interested, so I can hardly believe what the vet has told us, that he's not only deaf but nearly blind. When I call the vet to tell him how things are going he listens carefully, then says the last thing I want to hear. "I'm worried about those legs. If he's not using them in a month, you may want to reconsider your options." I go all limp and wobbly at this, but the vet goes right on in his matter-of-fact voice. "Meanwhile, just let him take the lead, go at his own rate. If he wants to get better, he'll let you know."

Let him take the lead, I tell myself after I've hung up. Fine. What could be more reasonable? But I worry about the legs, about the dog's not walking, and what will happen then.

One morning in early November about three weeks after the accident, I come down early to find the dog all the way across the kitchen, squatting in front of the back door. He is straining upright, his back legs still sprawled awkwardly on the floor, scrabbling feebly. He looks at me, then points his nose up toward the doorknob and cries to be let out. Taken aback, I open the door and watch as he struggles through the opening, the two hind legs pushing like flippers behind. He gets all the way out the door and several feet beyond before he gives up. As I pick him up to lug him the rest of the way, he grunts and his nose grazes back against my cheek, but he does not bite me. Outside on the grass I stand him on his feet and hold his back end, and for the first time he pisses standing up, the way he did at first when he was a puppy, before he learned to lift one leg. I remember one time in particular when he jerked his leg so high he over-balanced, fell backward, and caught himself right in the eye. The next time I take him out and hold him up, he takes two faltering steps forward before his rear end keels over onto the ground. But I'm elated; he's walking, or will be soon, and when I call the vet to tell him, he says, "That's a good sign; that's good."

All through the next month as fall turns into winter I lug the dog out, following behind with one hand on either side of his skinny rear, holding it up as he staggers along. The legs both work now, though he still drags one, but I can't let him go, because the weight of his hips on the tottery old legs gradually tilts over the weak side and he goes down, subsiding slowly over to the ground the way he did when he was small. Then I have to set him back up again, but he will walk as long as I hold on, so I trot along behind him like a child playing train, eventually going all over the yard while he sniffs the snow for gossip, until finally my back can't take it anymore and I concoct a kind of sling for under his belly. Watching me trot after him, holding the contraption up, Phil shakes his head and says, "That's the first time I ever actually saw someone going around with his ass in a sling."

After a while the dog is strong enough to get around with me hanging onto the tip of his tail as though it were a leash. My in-laws come to visit, and my father-in-law sneaks out early one morning, takes a picture of me in my bathrobe, down vest, and rubber snow boots trailing around behind the dog in the snow, holding his tail up like a plume. My mother-in-law comments, "Such devotion, I never would have believed it. You're certainly making it up to him. But don't your feet get cold?"

I shake my head, although they do, but that is little enough to pay for this miraculous recovery, little enough as expiation for my sins.

VII

"Well, old man," I hear Phil murmur as he lets the dog out one morning the next fall, "you may outlive me yet." The dog looks back at him, then staggers out and down the porch steps, rickety on his old pins, but no more than any sixteen-year-old arthritic dog, to do his morning rounds. He has, according to the vet, recovered as fully as possible from the accident, but the effects of old age, weak kidneys and arthritis are creeping up on him, and he is getting frailer. A bad liver infection he contracted in the spring did not help much, and he has had several fits in the last few months, which the vet regards as warning signs of progressive terminal kidney failure. He has told Phil that it is just a matter of time; most dogs his size don't live past twelve, let alone sixteen. When Phil asks him what to do, the vet shrugs, says we'll know when it's time, that we will be able to tell when his life is not worth living to him anymore. So we watch and wait, but so far it does not seem the time has come and we think we'll let him have this one last summer, and when winter comes, then it will be time. He is as he was, if frailer, and in fact in the late summer after we change his diet the fits come less frequently. He still seems pleased to be alive, and it seems he'll go on forever, in his contracted world. He does not go out of the yard now, and he can't get up the stairs to sleep under our bed the way he used to, falling to his belly with a crash and thumping on his elbows as far in as he could get. He sleeps downstairs now, on a blanket in the dining room next to my chair. He seems perfectly happy in this world of downstairs and around the yard, places he knows intimately by smell and feel, if no longer by sight and sound.

Anyway, it is Phil we're concerned with now. The tumor has recurred and the local doctors, at a loss, have at our insistence agreed to send Phil to a big cancer center in Boston to have his case reevaluated, to see if something can be done. The doctors here are worried about his kidneys—or rather kidney, since we now know that one was mistakenly removed during the operation in 1979. So Phil is home now, and we are waiting for a bed. When one is free, Phil's parents will come up to stay with the children, and Phil and I will drive to Boston. Phil is not hopeful, and thus his comment to the dog, not meant for anyone to hear. He knows I don't want to hear things like that, believing as always where there's life there's hope; his fatalism is balanced by my refusal, with what I consider to be ample precedent, to declare the game is over, at least in public and out loud.

Contemplating Phil's illness and what we have come to so soon, Phil not even forty yet, I see this as the apotheosis of a childhood fantasy, conceived not too long after my father died, while we were still living in Toledo, before my mother gave up on living by ourselves and we all moved back with my grandmother and my aunt in Skaneateles, in what I have come to think of as the house of widows.

In the street in back of us on River Road there was a big boy, a bully, head of a gang of children in a subdivision neighborhood—the Island Avenue gang. Although I played with many of the kids in the gang, I was never invited to belong, by virtue of my address as well as my timidity. The bully and his cohorts used to tease me unmercifully on the way home from school, and I was a natural and satisfactory victim, quick to respond and especially to cry. My mother told me I had to learn to fight my own battles, and the worst thing I could do was to talk back or cry. I must let them know they didn't bother me one bit. I was to turn the other cheek, as my father used to say, so one day I did just that, leaning back against the fence nonchalantly as they passed, chanting, "Sticks and stones will break my bones, but words will never hurt me," while rather prominently looking the other way. In an instant the bully had whipped off his leather belt and whacked me across the face with the buckle end. It laid the skin above my eye right open, narrowly missing my eyeball and, as my outraged mother later told the parents of the bully, nearly blinding me for life. Naturally I was forbidden ever to play with the Island Avenue hooligans again, those ruffians, and for a long time my mother drove me to school the long way around.

My fantasy was this: In one of my lonely walks through the woods of the abandoned filtration plant up the road, I would come upon the bully, laid out cold, having fallen from a high branch of one of the trees that had been allowed to grow up on the reserve. He lay there either unconscious or with a broken leg, or both. And of course it was up to me to save him, which I did in any number of ways, the most implausible of which involved my carrying him piggyback all the way to Island Avenue. The upshot always was that I would rescue him somehow, and become the heroine of the gang.

This, I now recognize, was the original formulation of my rescuer complex, a conversion into fantasy of my feeling that I should somehow have prevented my father's death, either by not letting him go away from home or by being there when the heart attack hit, so he'd know someone was there and wouldn't die. But I failed at this, and the conviction of my original powerlessness developed into an irresistible impulse to rescue everything and everyone in sight.

Certainly life has given me ample opportunity to exercise this impulse, but over the years I have gotten better at moderating it somewhat—take for instance my mother's last psychotic episode, in 1975, when she wound up in yet another paranoid frenzy in an Auburn motel. It was the seventh go-round since 1969—the second in a little over a year—and my sister had washed her hands of the whole thing and was on her way to Colorado. But instead of jumping in the car and driving ten hours to get there and take care of things, even though it was once again my turn, after pondering the problem for a while, I finally sent the motel owner a card with several phone numbers and the message: "In case of any trouble with Martha Gilead, please contact the following." Sure enough, three days later a social worker from the psychiatric ward at Auburn General called me with the news that my mother was there, they were putting her back on lithium, and everything was going to be just fine. We'd heard that many times before, but oddly enough this time they were right, or close enough. There have been one or two lapses since, but she has generally been getting better and better. She came through her mastectomy five years ago with no trouble, and even showed up unexpectedly when Phil was in the hospital for so long after his operation to help me with the kids, just like anybody else's mother. She's helping to put my sister Fran through medical school; last spring she took a bus down to see my brother and his family, and even went by herself into Philadelphia to see the Garden Show. She writes letters now which, if a little scrawly at times, are funny ha-ha, not funny peculiar, so that I sometimes feel I am getting glimpses of the way she must have been when she was young and first married to my father. I think I have a better understanding of what she must have gone through in her sad life, and it seems possible now that, after all these years, we may even have resumed that old uncomplicated childhood mother-daughter relationship so abruptly short-circuited nearly thirty years ago. So it seems that after all our combined efforts over the long haul, she is finally rescued for good.

But the situation with Phil makes all these other rescues seem like dress rehearsals, mere warm-ups. The doctors have told us he is dying, has perhaps six months, a year to live. If his words to the dog are any indication, he feels some parallel in their predicaments, though Phil is only thirty-nine, and the dog in people years is upwards of a hundred and two, and of course the dog is just a dog. But both of them are waiting for a sign that says, "It's time to give."

While we are waiting, we go about our business, to work, to school, or in Phil's case sailing, since he has taken a medical leave from the college. The days stretch on, the pathology reports crisscross the medical establishment, and one day I notice a growth in the dog's mouth that is interfering with his chewing. Since nothing else is going on at the moment, I load him in the car and take him to the vet's. It's the first time we've been there since his liver infection in the spring, and he quivers and trembles and looks pathetic, but acquiesces finally in his elderly dignified way.

This vet is horrified when he looks in the dog's mouth. "Oh, Jesus," he says, baring his teeth in a grimace of pained discovery. The growth is large and black, a piece of the dog's inner lip, looking like a giant slug of chewed-up licorice bubble gum. "Melanoma," the vet mutters. "Not good."

It doesn't sound good to me either. Melanoma is a cancer in humans, and a friend of ours has just died of it at the age of forty-one.

"Pretty advanced," the vet goes on. "He's probably got it other places. too. Why didn't you bring him in before?"

"Could it be something else?" I ask, ignoring his implication. The question's worked before. In fact, sometimes I think it works for everything except death itself.

"Nope," the vet says non-negotiably as he gets out his tools, a huge hypodermic and a vial. Suddenly I'm overtaken by a terrible suspicion.

"You're not going to put him to sleep, are you?"

"Of course," the vet says, holding up the vial and sucking the pale green fluid back into the huge needle.

"But, but . . ." I throw an arm protectively over the dog, who looks up at me curiously, the iridescent cataracts in his eyes catching the light, momentarily clouding the bright puppy look. "Just like that? But . . . but we haven't even discussed it," I say desperately. The fact is, I'm not ready for this.

"What's there to discuss?" the vet says imperturbably. "If I don't put him to sleep for this, he'll squirm all over. I don't think you can hold him. And I've felt those teeth too many times before."

I stare at the vet. Dumb. Put him to sleep. Right. For the operation. He's going to remove the growth and send us on our way, reprieved again. I nod, and he grabs a front leg, jabs the needle in while I hold the dog's nose.

But there is not even time for a struggle, the odd snap; as soon as the needle hits his skin the dog goes limp, without even time to shut his eyes, which roll back and shine dully up at me, sightless under peaky eyebrows. He looks dead, and I think in horror that the vet has killed him, either by accident or—knowing me—by design.

"Is he dead?" I gasp.

"Of course not," the vet says as he turns toward an instrument that resembles a blowtorch. "Just out cold."

The blowtorch thing is in fact an electric cauterization needle, and the vet burns away the tumor while I hold the dog, his body limp as a fur rug, his head lolling, the tongue hanging to one side like a slab of veal. I count his teeth; some are missing, some broken. Dogs should not outlive their teeth, I think, such an indignity. But he's got plenty left. "When will he wake up?" I want to know.

"In an hour or so. He'll be pretty shaky for a while. You got any errands downtown?" The vet hangs up the electric scalpel, finished. The growth is gone, or near enough. "I can't promise you much in the long run, though. These things are generally lethal," he says, looking at me seriously. "It won't be long. You might want to talk it over with your husband. It may be time."

But when I pick the dog up later that afternoon he's wide awake and frisky, still the same old dog with his foxy, handsome face. He skitters across the floor in his eagerness to get out of there, staggers out to the car and hops into his place in the front footwell, next to my feet, and home we go. I don't mention to Phil what the vet told me; there will be time to do that later when we get Phil squared away himself. The dog's all right for the time being, and it's not winter yet.

VIII

And the end of the story is this:

It's been almost two weeks since Phil and I drove down to Boston to the hospital, but all the tests are in now, and the operation is scheduled for tomorrow. It's old home week in Phil's room, doctors coming over from the Institute: surgeons, endocrinologists, oncologists, nephrologists, radiologists, anesthesiologists, not to mention nurses, nurse's aides, student nurses, all wanting to wish him well. He's very popular around here—someone they can cure, or hope they can. And the phone calls come in from all over, too: Maine, Vermont, New Jersey, California. His hometown doctor has called, some friends have called, his sisters have called.

Phil lies there, his cheeks pudgy from all the fluids they've pumped into him to offset the anticipated effects of tomorrow's surgery. He's also chockful of Valium, grinning cheerfully. Besides the doctors, two friends are visiting; it's a three-ring circus. I haven't been here very long myself; in fact, I just got in from Vermont after spending two days with Phil's parents and the kids.

Finally everyone leaves, and then the phone rings again. "You get it," Phil says. "I'm tired of talking." It's almost time for his body shave and the enema they've promised him to get his bowels whistle clean "just in case."

I pick up the phone. "Sara, is that you?" It's Phil's mother, and she sounds so upset I decide on the spot I'm not going to let her talk to Phil. But it's me she wants. "Listen, I'm sorry to bother you at a time like this, but it's about the dog. I don't know what's wrong, but he had a fit in the study and he's messed himself and all over the floor, poor soul, and he's lying in it and can't get up." In the background I can hear yelping and howling, shouting of several voices: Pop and the kids. "When we went to help him he tried to bite Pop," she finishes, her voice trailing off into a quaver. "We don't know what to do."

I stand there gripping the phone, thinking, I just don't believe it. The phone hums, the dog yelps, and I hear Pop's voice raised faintly: "No, no, don't go near him!"

The phone sniffles, clears its throat, waiting. "Sara?" I shut my eyes, my head buzzing angrily. They're asking *me* what to do, for chrissake? What do they expect, me to drive back up tonight and rescue the goddamned dog? Can't they deal with this themselves? It's the night before Phil's operation, and they can't cope with a stupid dog?

"I hate to bother you at a time like this," my mother-in-law repeats, "but we thought you should know."

For once I'm speechless.

"Sara?" my mother-in-law says timidly after a moment. Phil is looking at me, his head lifted off the pillow, alarmed. "The dog is sick," I say with my hand over the phone. "They're all hysterical." Phil's head flops back, his eyes closed. He looks relieved. "I thought it was one of the kids," he says.

Meanwhile, not used to being stuck for an answer, I'm thinking furiously. It's eight o'clock at night. The clamor at the other end of the phone squawks in my ear; all hell has broken loose. "Okay, look," I say as calmly as I can to Phil's mother. "If you're afraid to go near the dog, call Punch next door or Joyce up the street—the dog knows both of them— and ask them to come and help you. See if you can get him in the car and take him straight to the vet's. Then call me back. Call me back no matter what."

They call me back ten minutes later. Nobody's home, not Punch, not Joyce, not even the vet. "Well, just shut the doors and leave him until tomorrow morning," I say at last. "There's nothing else anybody can do."

"Poor soul," my mother-in-law says. "I feel so bad for him."

"There's nothing I can do," I tell her, unable to keep the exasperation out of my voice any longer.

"I know, Sara, I know," she says wearily. "We just

thought you ought to know. Can I speak to my son now?"

I hand the phone over to Phil, and that's the end of that.

Over the next couple of days I'm at the hospital constantly, during the eight hours of Phil's operation and his subsequent stay in the intensive care unit. I hardly think about the dog. When I call with the good news that the operation was an apparent success, they tell me almost as an afterthought that the man from the general store down the street came over the next morning to help Pop get the dog into the car, but at the last minute he got up and walked into the car under his own power, God bless him, so maybe things aren't so bad. But he cried all night, and they're all exhausted. They'll let me know what happens, and everything's under control.

Meanwhile, Phil is recovering but in a lot of pain, and both of us have to struggle with the horrors, remembering the other operation and its aftermath. But he amazes everyone with his rapid progess, his eagerness to get up and get going, back on his feet. I spend most of my time there. The nurses let me stay beyond the ten minutes at a time, because by now they know I won't scream and cry and faint into the forest of IVs and monitors around his bed, and besides, my presence seems to help. I don't cry at all; I haven't yet and I don't now, because things are looking up. One day runs into the next in ICU, but he makes rapid progress. One minute I am watching Phil, vacant-eyed and dopey, trying to stand up between two stocky nurses; the next time I see him he's walked around the whole unit and is talking about sending out for a pizza. The nurses joke about not knowing what to do for him since no one ever eats real food in ICU. But they are short of beds in the step-down unit where Phil goes next, and they want to keep him in here one more day. So I leave for Cambridge, thinking how relaxed and jolly it all is, and how everything is going so well.

But when I get back to our friends' house where I'm staying there's a message: "Call home." And it's the dog. The vet has called that morning, Sunday, to find out what we want to do. The dog is suffering, sick and retching, can't stand up. I'm supposed to call him. "His life is a misery to him," my mother-in-law says sadly, and I can guess what it is the vet wants me to say. And so I call the vet.

"The dog is really in bad shape, full of tumors, advanced kidney failure," he says in his matter-of-fact, professional, but not unsympathetic voice. "There's no point in prolonging this. I hate to see him suffer this way."

He wants my permission; all I have to do is say the word—two words, actually: Do it. And I remember the times Phil and I talked about this, how we would want to be there, and my throat dries up and my tongue cleaves to the roof of my mouth, and I can't say anything at all.

"I've got to think about it," I say finally. "I don't know what to do." I explain to the vet what's going on down here, Phil still in Intensive Care, that I can't leave right now.

"He wouldn't know you," the vet says. "He's really out of it, doesn't know much of anything any more." He pauses, waiting. "But it's entirely up to you."

Still I can't do it. I try to remember the last time I saw the dog, whether I even noticed him, patted him and said good-bye. It's a familiar feeling, this guilt, and I have to remind myself he's just a dog.

"I've got to think it over," I say finally in my crabbed voice, aware of the vet's silent disapproval on the other end. He thinks that this is sentimental bullshit, and in a way it is. "I can't decide now, I just can't," I tell him apologetically. "Let me sleep on it, and I'll call you in the morning."

And then I go to bed, but I don't sleep, and in fact this is the worst night I've spent since we came down to Boston. Somehow the dog's trouble has gotten lost in all this other business, but he's been such a good old friend and can it be there's no time to spare after all these years to see him out? I toss and turn, arguing with myself he's just a dog, he wouldn't know I was there, it's silly, stupid, a waste of time and energy. In the midst of all this, I remember the time not long ago when I took him in to have the growth removed and thought the vet had killed him, that he was dead just like that, right before my eyes. And I think that is how it would be, the first shot that puts him out instantaneously, with no pain, and then the second one that stops the heart. He'll never know what hit him. Not a bad death, so quick, so humane, and how can it be worth it for me to drive all the way back up there just for those few seconds? And have I made it up to him, I wonder in the dark? Did I really make him better, and was it worth it to him, even though it's come to this? And all the time I'm thinking this, I know it's not the dog I need to rescue; it's me.

In the morning I've made up my mind. I'm driving up. I call the hospital to get a report on Phil; he's been moved out of Intensive Care, his condition satisfactory, stable. I dial the vet's number to let him know I'm coming.

And the vet says, "I'm afraid it's out of your hands. The dog passed away in his sleep last night. I found him this morning. So it's all been decided for you."

"Thanks," I croak, barely able to hang up the phone. I cross over to the couch, bury my face in my hands, and start to cry—sudden loud, wet, uncontrollable sobs.

"Oh, my God!" my friend Jane shrieks as she stops dead in the doorway of the room, her hands flying to her face in a pantomime of anticipated horror. "Oh, my God, Sara! Oh, no! What's happened, what's wrong?"

Of course, seeing me crying, she thinks it's Phil. I look up at her, damp and trembling with these my first, my only, and my ancient tears, and say, "No, it's all right. It's just the dog. It's just the goddamned dog."

And this is what I've learned about the dead: It is not always their absence that haunts us. So I still hear the clink of a chain collar against a porcelain bowl, the skittering of toenails across a wooden floor, the thump and sigh of a weary dog flopping his old bones down next to my chair. I feel the presence of those old bones under my chair, under my feet. Under my wheels.